AND THEN THERE WAS

CHERYL BARTON

Published by: Cheryl Barton Publishing, LLC

Cheryl Barton Publishing, LLC
P.O. Box 962
Reisterstown, Maryland 21136
www.crbarton.com

Ordering Information:
Quantity sales.
Special discounts of this novel are available on quantity purchases by corporations, associations, and others. For details, contact the publisher at the address above.

Orders by U.S. trade bookstores and wholesalers. Please contact prez@crbarton.com

ISBN: 1948950103
ISBN-13: 978-1-948950-10-7

Dear Reader,

I recently returned from an incredible trip to Hollywood, California and while there, I explored and ended up in Malibu. I enjoyed the beach, drove up Pacific Coast Highway (a dream of mind), checked out a few great restaurants and loved the beautiful homes that lined the coastline. I was inspired to write a Malibu themed romance series from the impact and the majesty of the beauty I encountered. Love can be discovered anyplace, but I wanted to take time to focus on a city that I came to love in a short period of time. I hope you enjoy book one of my new *"Malibu Hearts"* series and that you will stick around for the four follow-up novels that are coming!

First up is, *"And Then There Was You,"* a beautiful, sexy love story, set in Malibu, California and focuses on the growing love between Diezel Wilder, an attorney from New York who recently moved to California after a bitter divorce from a woman he married on a whim and Brooklyn Hunter, a sexy Armenia bombshell, who is a late-night, on-air radio talk show host who woos men all over the country with her sexy, sultry, seductive voice. Brooklyn is coming off of a divorce from a man twenty years older, who she thought was helping her escape a dismal existence only to thrust her into the Hollywood spotlight which revealed adultery and out of wedlock children. Seeking a new lease on life, Diezel and Brooklyn are in search of the kind of connection with a mate that leaves you breathless. Little did they know they would find it right next door. Bring on the ice-cold water because you're about to go on one very steamy ride to love in, *"And Then There Was You."*

Happy Reading!

Cheryl

Acknowledgement

Many years ago, someone offered my mother a bag of romance novels to give to me since I had always been an avid reader. When she asked me if I wanted the books, I declined because I wasn't into romance novels, all that mushy stuff, which is what I said at the time. I was more into reading mystery, spy and espionage novels by Robert Ludlum, Tom Clancy, Jonathan Kellerman and Stephen King. Me reading that spicy, sexy stuff? I turned my nose up at it.

Years later, I picked up a romance novel in a dollar store. I would often find great mystery books marked down at a big discount and one day, I saw the cover of a romance novel and for a dollar, I decided, why not. I read that book in one day and then I couldn't get enough. I found my love for reading romance and I ended up buying ten to fifteen books a week, hence the large paperback collection I still have today.

My love for reading romance led me to African American romance authors and what came next? You got it, my love for writing romance was birthed. Even though I didn't accept those romance novels and I still regret that to this day, even still, my love for romance novels thrived. I want to say thank you to my mother because the day I read and fell in love with reading romance, reminded me of years of what I missed out on because I didn't accept those books. Trust me, I've made up for it with the number of romance novels I still read today!

Before that, I loved reading since I was very young and my love for books of all type came from watching my father who also loved and still does love reading.

Here I am today, not only still an avid reader of crime, mystery, espionage, spy and science fiction novels, but I love reading sexy, spicy romance novels and more than anything, I love writing them. The ideas come faster than I can write them, but I'm thankful that with each day comes another opportunity to pen another romance novel. Thanks mom and dad for my love of all things books!

1

Malibu nights in California were quiet, tranquil, serene and Brooklyn Hunter tended to forget the outside world to appreciate the still of the night. She loved the exquisite view from her home, marveling at the most beautiful sight of the ocean from her one in a million, vantage point on the hillside overlooking the sandy Malibu beach. She loved every opportunity she got to sit back and relax in her four-bedroom oceanfront home where she could gaze up at the dark blue sky with its well-lit moon reflecting off of the waters of the Pacific Ocean. Brooklyn never felt more at peace than she did being at home without the distracting sound of the television or radio especially since most nights, she was at work at a local radio station hosting her own late-night talk show on satellite radio.

What she missed while she was at work was time spent luxuriating on her U-shaped, butter yellow, plush, fabric sectional which faced the glass doors that led to her large wrap-around white wooden deck. The view of the calm waters was perfect as they moved slowly back and forth showing the majesty that was an ocean of blue. This is what she always thought her life should be and not the circus that she'd lived for a large part of her adult life. At the age thirty, she hadn't lived much of her adult life yet, but she'd experienced more than most people. Married at twenty-two to a forty-five-year-old Hollywood studio executive and then divorced at twenty-seven after years of scandal and living her life in the spotlight, she appreciated her current state of no more drama.

Tucking her feet under her as she picked up the glitter stemmed glass of her favorite white wine, Brooklyn thought about how far she'd come in her thirty years and she was thankful that though she'd made some mistakes, her life was focused on her. She smiled realizing she still had a lot of years to make new ones. For now, she was taking life one uneventful day after another and inwardly gave thanks that she now felt freer than she had in a long time.

Unexpectedly and interrupting the quietness of the night, she heard a sound that made her pause all movement and thought. Sitting extremely still in her dim-lit family room, the only room in the house she'd had a light on in, she listened and thought maybe she'd been so focused on her thoughts that she'd imagined she heard something when she really hadn't. Noticing nothing but the still of the night again, she relaxed back, but that only lasted a few seconds. She heard another sound and this time she was sure it was coming from right outside of her house, possibly on the part of her deck that ran along the side of the house.

It wasn't often she heard anything on either the deck that surrounded two sides of her house or even on the brick front walkway that led to her front door and attached garage. Tonight, her peace was invaded causing her to stand and listen as if standing was going to increase her audible sensors.

Brooklyn jumped when she again heard movement and this time, it sounded like it was coming from under one of the four large paned windows with a view of her neighbor's house, currently covered with blinds that were drawn. She walked closer to where she heard the noise and listened. Again, she heard what appeared to be movement of some sort, faint, but she still heard it.

"Hello?" Brooklyn heard the echo of her own voice as it bounced off of the walls. People would often tell her that they loved the sound of her voice as they listened to the overnight satellite radio broadcast of her popular, *"Bring the Real, Realness"* talk show. Hearing her own voice, she didn't understand the fascination with it.

She was told the deep, smoky, raspy sound of it was sexy and brought chills to both men and women alike every time she signed on and off with her signature phrase, *"this is Brooklyn Hunter, dimming the light on the real, realness until we meet again"*. Perhaps because she was a little frightened, she didn't sound sexy at all. She didn't even know why she was focused on the sound of her voice when there could be someone lurking around the outside of her house. There was a time that she was stalked by paparazzi, but now that she lived a life outside of the Hollywood glitz and glamour, she rarely saw anyone skulking around her or her house. She felt secure indoors as long as she kept the alarm on, pretty sure no one could get inside of the house, but that didn't diminish her thoughts that blended her reality with that of the horror movie she'd watched the night before. Clearly, that had been a mistake. Living alone and watching horror movies late do not make for a peaceful night. She was scaring herself in a home that she knew was secure enough to keep anyone out she didn't want in.

Her stunning two-story beachfront contemporary home was private and elegant with magnificent panoramic ocean, island and coastline views. It was located near the Malibu-Santa Monica border and has private access to the beach used only by those who lived along her strip which consisted of roughly thirty properties.

After purchasing the house, she'd had it remodeled throughout with Roman Coliseum style beams and woodwork along with dark brown hardwood floors. Her appliances were all top-of-the-line and state of the art with more gadgets, bells and whistles than she knew how to operate. She loved the large open floor plan that combined her living room, dining room and family room all into one large space. There was also a spare bedroom and one full and one-half bath on the first level. The feature she loved the most was the three walls of windows that allowed the sun to shine through whenever she opened the blinds and curtains.

The second level consisted of three bedrooms, each with their own ensuite bathroom. The house also included a two-car garage with two additional car ports, giving her plenty of space to park her two cars, a Maserati and her new Jeep Wrangler. On her days off, she loved taking her jeep for long rides into the mountains. The sound she heard came from the area behind the garage and along the side of the house where her property was divided from the one next door. She jumped again when she heard a scratching noise.

Peering out of one of the windows, she saw no one but could hear a sound. The lighting around the perimeter of her property didn't light up as it should if someone was out there, adding to her assessment that maybe she was hearing things. She'd had a long day, but she wasn't tired or weary.

Checking the cameras that pointed to all sides of her property, especially the back where there was access to her house from the beach, she finally saw something as she tried to stretch her eyes to focus better on what it was.

"Is that a dog?" she asked herself. It wasn't often that she saw a dog roaming free in Malibu. She watched the little pup as it sniffed around the base of her house before coming around toward her sliding glass door.

Brooklyn turned on a low light which seemed to temporarily scare the puppy. When she smiled, it yipped and jumped and she went to open the door. As soon as she turned the alarm off and opened it, the puppy came closer and sniffed her.

"Who are you and where did you come from?" she said looking around for a possible owner.

Noticing a collar, she checked it and found a tag with a note. She read it out loud as if the dog would understand.

"His name is Denim and if found, return to the Wilders."

Brooklyn knew exactly who the owner was. It had to be Davis Wilder, the movie producer who lived next door.

"When did he get a dog since he's never at home?" she asked herself out loud.

She talked to him as she rubbed behind his ears. Her heart melted when he snuggled close and whatever direction she moved her hand, he moved his head to make sure she didn't stop rubbing in his furry coat.

"You sure are friendly, but I'm sure Davis is wondering where you are or he will be. I thought he was out of the country for the next six months. Anyway, let's get you home," she said.

Opening her front door, she closed it behind her and rushed next door across the large flat bricks that made a path between the two properties. She was happy that the beach front properties were only a few feet away from each other. She loved Malibu and considered it pretty safe, but living alone, she still liked being indoors at night.

She coddled the puppy as he moved around happily in her arms as they walked up to the door. Ringing the bell, she waited for Davis to answer wondering if he was even home. Though she thought he was away, whenever he was home, he loved parking his customized Range Rover in the driveway since the two spaces inside usually housed one of his other cars or his girlfriend, Delaney's, Mercedes Coupe. He must not know that his dog was out roaming around close to eleven at night. She turned briefly to look at the cars passing on Pacific Coast Highway when she heard the door open. As she turned, ready to smile up at Davis' six-five height, her smiled turned to shock when Davis wasn't the person who stood on the other side of the door. As if she didn't know where she was, she leaned back and checked the address again and then felt foolish when she did. She had only walked next door and she knew whose house it was.

"Hi," she said holding the puppy up and out to the man on the other side of the glass door. She wanted to say more, but any additional words were cut off in her throat as her eyes locked onto a man who was too handsome for words. He stood in front of her in a white tank top that showed bulging, muscled, rugged biceps which flexed everywhere from his massive arms to what she knew was a chiseled chest and flat, toned stomach underneath. For a split second, she started to ask if he was the actor known as 'The Rock' because the mystery man looked like he could play his stunt double. Two real-life twins couldn't look more alike than this man and the famous actor.

"Hi there," he said to her and then turned his attention to the puppy. "Denim, what are you doing outside?" he said opening the glass door and stepping outside as the puppy yipped away excitedly is if he was just coming back from the war after being gone for months.

Brooklyn had yet to say anything other than hello and she felt stupid when her mouth wouldn't move. She couldn't stop looking at how handsome he was and where was Davis? This stranger resembled him and she had a feeling they were at least related. When he reached for the pup who happily jumped from her arms to his and proceeded to lick his face already apologizing for apparently getting out, she thought of how lucky that puppy was getting the chance to lick on all that deliciousness. She shook off the image of being in his arms with her mouth all over him as she cleared her throat of the invisible blockage and her mind of her lascivious thoughts. Finally, she'd found her voice to express more than just hello.

"Hello. I'm Brooklyn and I was expecting Davis. I live right next door," she pointed, "and this beauty here was wandering around my property and ended up at the glass doors to my deck. I saw the name Wilder on his tag and I know Davis' last name is Wilder," she explained.

"I'm Diezel and Denim here has been a bad boy, I see," he said, nuzzling him.

Diezel finally looked at his neighbor for more than just a second and forgot that the world was spinning. He was suddenly star-struck the moment his eyes settled on Brooklyn Hunter, a woman he's admired and secretly lusted after from a distance for a long time. He had no idea his brother lived next door to her. Since he had recently moved from New York and hadn't visited Davis' house in Malibu in a few years, he didn't know who lived next door. He couldn't believe his luck that he'd been asked to keep an eye on the house for six months while Davis was out of the country and while the house he'd recently purchased for himself in Los Angeles was being remodeled.

"It's nice to meet you," she said.

"I'm Davis' better looking much younger brother," he smiled and extended his hand for a handshake. When he should have let go, he didn't because a surge of familiarity shot from her to him like a bolt of hot, sexiness amped up higher by her beauty. He didn't want to let her hand go, but did so to avoid any strange behavior on his part.

"Davis has spoken of you several times," she said. "In fact, he mentioned all of his brothers and sister, but I've only met one of you. I haven't seen him for a few weeks," she added.

"He's out of the country working on a film for the next six months or so. He left a few weeks ago, a bit earlier than he'd planned and I'll be house sitting while he's gone. It's nice to meet you. I listen to your satellite broadcast show in the evenings and I'm a fan," he said and hoped that he didn't come across as a stalker or obsessed fan, knowing she probably had many. He didn't say whether he was a fan of her or the show when in fact the answer was, both.

"You recognized me?" she asked and smiled. "Most people don't since it's my voice they hear every night and not my face they see," she added.

"I would recognize your beauty anywhere and that raspy voice is unmistakable and even better in person. I bet you get compliments all the time. The sound of your voice is unique."

"I do especially when people see me and try to put the voice with the face," she acknowledged.

"Looks like we'll be neighbors for at least six months. I'm sorry about Denim here. He's quite the escape artist, I see. I'll have to keep a closer eye on him until my daughter gets here. She would go ballistic if she got here and Denim wasn't here to greet her. I promised her I would watch him with my life and after only a few days, I've failed miserably," he joked.

"Well, he didn't go far."

"I guess he wanted to check out the beautiful woman next door and I don't blame him."

Brooklyn wanted to reply, but she couldn't stop blushing.

"Thank you. So, you'll be living here for a while?" she asked. The hour was late and Brooklyn knew that she should get back home on one of only two nights off she gets each week. Right now, her show aired five nights a week at midnight, Tuesday through Saturday. She was planning on binge watching all of her favorite shows after a tiresome week of doing her show and also out during the day doing promotions and appearances.

"I will. I recently moved to Los Angeles for work and a fresh start and the house I bought is being remodeled. I was planning to stay at one of Davis' other houses, but when he said he'd be leaving the country for a few months and the timing worked out, he thought I could use some of this beach life and I agreed. I've only been here a few days and I'm already hooked."

"Yes, the beach was the main selling point for me when I moved here three years ago."

Diezel understood. He couldn't seem to get enough of gazing out over the beach, day and night.

"I see why. Even at night, it's beautiful. I can already tell I'm going to miss this when I move into my house, though with Davis' crazy schedule, I'm sure I'll have plenty of time to hang out here when I want," he said.

"Well, I look forward to seeing you again. I'm going to head back over to my house. If you need anything, including a sitter for this beauty, just knock. It was night meeting you, Diezel." She then turned to Denim. "You, who planned, but didn't quite carry out the great escape, no more running away to the neighbor's house," she said rubbing his nose as he licked her hand. "I love Yorkies. One day when I'm home long enough to really give one attention, I'd love to get one," she said.

"Let me know. I have a friend who breeds pure bred Yorkies and sells them at a great price. I'm going to go check how he was able to get out of his cage. I put it on the back deck thinking he would love the fresh air off of the water and somehow, he got out and probably went down the back steps. All this time, I thought he was sleeping after our exhausting day of unpacking. Thanks for bringing him home. My daughter will be here in a few days and I would be toast if I had to tell her he got out and I couldn't find him."

"I'm glad I was able to help. Welcome to the neighborhood, even if it's only for a few months."

"I appreciate that. Maybe I'll see you soon on the beach," Diezel said and was already imagining her in a stringed bikini. She definitely had the body for it in the way he tried to catch glimpses of it while they talked. He was definitely going to enjoy housesitting next door to one of the world's most beautiful women.

"That's where I am two to three days a week. I love the water. I love going for a swim to clear my head especially after my show. Say hello if you come down to the beach and you see me," she said and walked back toward her own door. She turned after opening the outside door and waved to Diezel who had walked further out onto his property to see that she got inside.

Once inside, she closed the door and leaned back against it, exhaling the breath she'd been holding in.

"Whew, what a man," she said out loud.

2

Diezel spent the day unpacking a few more of his things. Between his time at the office getting acquainted with the west coast staff and checking on the work being done to his own recently purchased home in Los Angeles, he was beginning to feel like a stranger in the beach house. He seemed to only end up there when it was time to sleep. Thankfully, he didn't have to furnish the beach house or worry about bringing in a lot of other supplies because Davis' house was fully furnished and had all of the essentials anyone would need. Most of what he was unpacking were his clothes and clothes and other items for the room he was decorating for his daughter when she arrived for the summer.

His few days at the office had been exhausting, though he hadn't actually started working yet. He had recently received a promotion to partner in the law firm he had been working for in New York. With his move to California, lots of things had changed, but he was looking forward to the new lease on life he was creating for himself.

He walked over and looked out over the ocean.

Living in New York most of his life, he didn't see an ocean that looked anything like the one on the west coast and his neighbor had already begun invading his thoughts over the past few nights since she'd shown up at his door with Denim in hand. He'd seen pictures of her and listened to her show at night and still he wasn't prepared for the provocative visual upon seeing her.

Brooklyn was sexy from head to toe and her pleasant disposition had him longing for another chance encounter. Everything about her shouted awareness, making sure he didn't forget one thing about her and he hadn't. He was hoping to see her again, but in the past few days, they must have been missing each other. His cellphone rang turning his attention from her beauty to his ringing phone.

"Davis! What's up, bro!" he said happily. He hadn't heard from Davis since right before he flew to California.

"Did you find everything okay?" Davis asked.

"I did, but I'm pissed at you right now, like seriously pissed!" Diezel yelled into the phone. Hearing him shout brought Denim out of one of the two bedrooms on the first level of the two-level house. There were two more bedrooms on the upper level, one being Davis' main bedroom suite and the other being a guest room. Sitting down on the leather sofa, he picked Denim up and placed him on his lap.

"You're pissed? What are you angry about and

whatever it is, I didn't do it. I'm across the world – what could I have done?" Davis asked.

"You didn't tell me you lived next door to Brooklyn Hunter," he said. "Brooklyn Hunter!" he expressed again, stressing her name.

"Diezel, I live next door to Brooklyn Hunter. Happy now?" Davis asked mischievously.

"Oh, you're clown-funny today I see. You're lucky you are on the other end of the world someplace. Do you have any idea how fine Brooklyn Hunter is and adding in that voice, do you even know what the sound of that woman's voice does to men all over the country? I can't believe you didn't tell me she lived right next door!" he exclaimed.

"You have a thing for Brooklyn? How was I supposed to know that? You've never said anything. You have been trying to regroup after your divorce and the only focus you've had is on Daniella. How is my niece doing and when is she joining you? She still coming for the whole summer?" Davis asked.

Diezel smiled thinking of his daughter, Dani. His marriage may not have survived more than five years, but out of that time, the most precious jewel to him was born and at four years old, she already had him wrapped tightly around her finger.

"Dani is fine and will be here Sunday. I'll have two weeks of just hanging out with her before I start work at the new firm. Jessica originally planned on flying with her and turning right back around and heading back to New York, but instead, she called me last night to tell me that I needed to fly into New York to pick Dani up, which is not a problem. Jess would try anything to make it difficult for Dani to spend the summer here with me in California, but that's fine. As soon as I ended the phone conversation, I booked a flight to New York with a few hours layover time in case she comes up with another story."

"You know, you need to get custody of Dani. She would love living in Los Angeles. Jessica is a good mother, but you're a better father and I mean no disrespect of Jessica. Why should she be the one to get custody because she's the mother?" Davis asked.

"I hear you and I've thought about it, but I don't want to take Dani away from Jessica like that. I made the decision to move to Los Angeles knowing it would be a major adjustment. I will miss her like crazy, but every second I have where I can get away, I'll be flying back and forth to New York. Now that I'm a partner, the firm is assigning me to clients on the east coast so that I can fly back and forth and have time to see Dani during the school year. It'll be rough, but I'll make it work. You know I had to get out of New York. Jessica was making life hard for me, showing up everywhere, even at the office with a bunch of drama."

"I hear you. She's bitter and didn't appreciate you when she was married to you and then wanted to try and ruin your life. A good start is a great thing and I'm glad you'll be closer to me even though I'm gone more than I'm home. I am going to fly back for a few days next month. I'm thinking we call Dalton and Dietrick and make plans for all of us brothers to hang out in Malibu for a few days together and catch up. It's been years since we've been in the same place at the same time."

"I like that idea. Plus, Dani will get to see all of her uncles, which she will get a kick out of. Is Lanie coming with you?" Diezel asked. He knew that Davis' girlfriend Delaney traveled with him, especially when he traveled for long periods of time. He turned his face up when he heard Davis sigh on the other end and hesitate in responding.

"She's going to stay here. We were here one day and she was asked to model in a show. She's going to be tied up with that. Besides, by the time she packs everything under the sun just to fly back home as if she doesn't have clothes there, I'll be exhausted dealing with tons of luggage."

Something else was going on, Diezel thought. He would let it go for now, but the sound of Davis' voice and the way he responded told him his brother wasn't being totally honest.

"Cool and thanks for letting me use the house. This is definitely better than that monstrosity of a house you have in Calabasas. I think I would lose Dani if we were at that house with the ten bedrooms. Why a single guy needs a house with ten bedrooms that he's hardly ever in I don't know. Must be all that money you can't wait to spend," he joked.

"Haha, could be. You know I like to keep up with other studio producers."

"I get it – you want to show that yours is bigger?" Diezel joshed.

"Whatever. Anyway, don't slobber all over my neighbor and hands off. I know you when you see a beautiful woman," Davis suggested.

"Davis, have you seen your neighbor? Again, that voice, that body and just everything about her. I listen to her show sometimes at night and I've never heard a woman talk so comfortably about love and sex. It's definitely her lane. I never thought I would get the opportunity to meet her."

"Don't mistake a persona on the radio with who a woman really is. I'm not saying that to say anything negative about Brooklyn, I'm just saying. She is beautiful, but you already sound like you're smitten and you what, just met her? When did you meet her? She has crazy hours. We watch out for each other's homes."

At the mentioning of her name, a picture of her beautiful face surfaced in his mind and he smiled.

"Denim got out of his cage the other day. I had him in one on the back deck so that he could enjoy the night air. He found his way to her deck and she brought him over. I couldn't believe when I opened my door and she stood there holding him in her arms."

"She is definitely a bombshell. I think she's Armenian," Davis said.

"She can definitely pass for one of the Kardashian sisters. You know how I love a shapely woman and she's intelligent? That's the perfect woman and you know it," Diezel said.

"Right and that's why you and Jessica didn't work out. You went after her because of her looks and you didn't think about getting to know her. I'm thankful for my niece, but I hate that her mother takes you through a lot of drama. The next woman should be someone you get to know before jumping her bones. How about that?" Davis wisecracked.

"You know I can't resist a beautiful woman, but you're right that I went after Jessica because of her looks and she was wild in bed, but that was it and it took me a long time to realize that. We never had anything to talk about and barely had anything in common. Don't assume I'm already contemplating hopping in bed with Brooklyn. If anything, she's the kind of woman a man takes his time to get to know. Unlike you, I believe a big part of who she is, is in her radio show. She has the most popular late-night on-air talk show on the radio and trust me, people listen in because she's real. She's making men and women listen to what other women and men are really thinking and feeling and I respect and admire that," Diezel said.

"Do you know the history about her? One thing I've

learned living next door to her is that she is an incredible woman and I would never slight her when it comes to that. Like you, she's had her own share of drama and perhaps she's still vulnerable. She and Lanie have become close and I think a few times when Lanie is about to lose her mind dealing with me, Brooklyn helps to reign her back in with the same kind of logic she gives to her late-night callers. She can spit the knowledge because she's been on the other end of getting hurt. She's lived next door to me for three years and though I travel a lot, when I'm home, I haven't seen any men over there and Lanie has mentioned the same thing. She said they talked and Brooklyn has pretty much given up on the male species after what that studio executive she was married to did to her. She was deeply hurt, crushed even and yet she still rises and gets the job done. I'm not sure she's looking to be involved, but if you think differently, by all means go for it. If you hurt her, I will kill you. I still live next door to her and I don't want her to see me and remember that my baby brother hurt her like other men have done," Davis said.

"You said a lot and I hear you. I haven't made any kind of move and all I said was that I had met her, I love her show and she's gorgeous. I saw her early this morning running along the water's edge on the beach and it was like watching an episode of Baywatch in slow motion. I couldn't take my eyes away. I promise I'm not out to hurt anyone after what I went through with Jessica. Any woman I decide to get involved with won't be just to warm my bed and walk away. Definitely not if it's Brooklyn."

"Don't bed my neighbor, Diezel. You with those muscles and hazel eyes tantalizing and enticing women everywhere. Anyone ever tell you that you don't look like an attorney? You look like a wrestler."

"You mean besides you and my brother's who've been telling me that practically all of my life? You know I get that all the time, but then I hit them with intelligent words and a bunch of legal jargon and shock the hell out of them!" he laughed.

"Alright, mister corporate attorney, I'm out. Kiss Dani for me when she arrives and try not to get into a spat with Jessica at the airport."

"I'm planning to fly in and then take Dani for lunch before our flight out to keep down the tension with Jessica. Dani doesn't need to hear her mother raving like she does. I'm good. I'll let her call you when she gets here. You know she's gonna ask where you're at. I've been telling her all about your house on the beach. You know how much my daughter loves the water."

"Kiss her for me and call anytime. Don't forget there is a cleaning service if you want to use it and there is a guy who does all the landscaping every Saturday morning. I also have linen service and that's up to you to use or not. If you're not going to use it, the number is on the fridge. Call and let them know. It makes my life easier and you may find it easy too as you try to balance work and Dani every day. They'll also pickup your dry-cleaning and deliver it back to the house. They don't have access to the house, so when you're not there, the shed on the side of the house is what they have a key to. You'll find any deliveries in there."

"Wow, you are definitely the super-duper producer, living the high-life of a superstar. I'm good doing my own laundry!" Diezel proclaimed.

"Don't knock it, little brother. We're all benefiting from my high-life, don't forget. Have you heard from our sister? She is on break from college and supposed to be staying with Dalton. She told me she wants to move in with me, but I'm gone so much that I don't think that would be a good idea. She's twenty and still smelling herself," Davis said.

"I know. I talked to her last week. She was packing up her apartment for the summer and heading home to Florida. I'm thinking of letting her come to live with me when my house is done. I don't like her bouncing around all the time and I know she loves the west coast. What better place for her to be in than Los Angeles as she pursues an acting or modeling career. I'll keep you posted. Mom and dad would expect us to look out for her. I miss them," Diezel said somberly.

"We all miss them and I think about them every single day. They would be proud at how well we're all doing. Let me know what you plan to do. I don't mind her moving to the west coast, but we need to sit her down and talk about ground rules," Davis asserted.

"Ground rules? She's twenty and strong-minded like we've raised her to be. She'll turn those ground rules against you and tell you where to stick them. You know our baby sister. As long as she stays in school, let's not push her too hard. She's a good girl, still making the dean's list and we want to keep her that way," Diezel suggested.

"I hear you. I don't want her getting to California and turn all LaLa land on us."

"That's not her and you know it. I'll talk to her and see where her head is. We've all been through a lot, especially her with losing parents at a critical point in her life. I don't want anything pushing her away from us. I love how close we all are and how she knows she can come to us for anything. Let me handle this one and I'll keep you posted. Be safe over there and we'll talk in a few days."

"Good luck with Brooklyn," Davis said.

"It's been a few days and all I did was meet her. You're already suggesting something between us and you shouldn't," Diezel tried to explain and sound convincing. He already knew Davis wasn't buying it.

"I hear you and I don't hear you. Talk to you soon," Davis said and hung up.

Diezel shook his head at the thought of him and Brooklyn being involved and waved it off. He had no doubt she was most likely involved with someone.

Just because Davis didn't know or see who it was doesn't mean there wasn't someone. Lucky guy if so, he thought.

Changing his thoughts from Brooklyn, he decided to shower, change and walk out on the beach after taking Denim for a walk in the area where dogs were allowed.

As he moved about the house, his thoughts turned to their parents who were killed in an accident with a tractor trailer over five years ago. They had been heading back to New York where the family lived and a truck driver, who had exceeded the number of miles he should have been driving without a break, fell asleep at the wheel and ran them off the road down an embankment. From what they were, before their car burst into flames, they had both died from the impact of the car rolling down the hill. Since then, he and his three brothers have looked after their sister, Delia, who, back then at the age of fifteen, had a hard time adjusting to them being gone. They all did, but the five of them were close and always looked out for each other.

Following the accident and lawsuit filed on their behalf, they each received a substantially large financial settlement, with more going to their sister who would receive hers when she turned twenty-five and had graduated college. Though she could receive a hefty stipend each month, the brothers each opted to have her trust fund untouched and they took care of everything she wanted and needed.

The brothers each took less of the settlement and added more to her settlement while Davis didn't take any. Instead, he spread his settlement out amongst the other siblings because he was already very well off as a high-profile movie producer. Nothing and no amount of money could take the place of parents, who loved and adored all five of them equally and unconditionally. He missed them every day.

Looking down, Denim crawled around his feet, his sign that he wanted to go out.

"Okay, buddy. Let's go for a walk. Dani will be here soon and she'll be happy to see you. I know you can't wait to see her. Let's go out and enjoy some of this sunshine."

Finding his leash, he followed Denim to the front door where he jumped around excited to know the door was about to open and he could break free without sneaking out.

3

"Good evening lovies, this is your host, Brooklyn Hunter. It's midnight and you know what that means – it's time to start tonight's broadcast of *"Bring the Real, Realness"*, my nightly talk show where I'm just as much of an audience to you as you are to me. I want to thank the millions of listeners who tune in each and every night to share their personal experiences with me while I give you some of my truth, too. As you know, I'm not shy about sharing who I am and what my desires are as a woman. We share and share alike around these parts. Women, keep on being real with me and the men in your life. They won't know if you don't say so, right? Men, thanks for being a large part of my audience, too. I love how you want to explain what makes you tick and you keep it real with the ladies. This show is successful because we bring the real, realness to life situations and I hope what we learn is as helpful to you as it is to me. We're all in this thing called life and love together. We're going to kick off tonight with our usual, *Sexual Healing*, from Marvin Gaye and then I'll be back on with our first topic of the night which his, would you rather be wanted or needed in a relationship? Let's get some music poppin' and I'll be back in a flash."

Brooklyn put on the song and leaned back as her assistant entered the studio.

"Hey, Robin! Ready for another interesting night?" she asked.

Robin Walters had been her on-air assistant since she began the show a few years back and she has since become even more of a friend. Robin walked over and sat in the seat opposite Brooklyn and opened up her book to check the lineup for topics for the night.

"I sure am and I see we have some spicy subjects for discussion tonight. Is it me or are these a little juicier than usual? What has your panties all steamed up tonight? You've been pretty tame lately, but last night and tonight, you seem to be focusing on something or somebody. What gives and don't try to lie because I've learned what your lying face looks like – you know that look you try to give me when you don't want me to know the real answer?"

Brooklyn shuffled in her seat and looked in any direction other than directly at Robin.

"We're about to go back on line. Let's talk later," she said, happy to be able to avoid any talk about what's going on with her. She didn't want to share that her focus was on her sexy neighbor and had been since she'd met him. Diezel. She said his name in her head and sighed with exuberance. No woman would be able to get her mind off of all that gorgeousness.

"Wait, does that mean you'll tell me the truth later or does it mean you're going to take the next few hours and come up with a good lie?" Robin kidded.

"Truth. I got you," Brooklyn winked and then put her headset back on as they settled in for the night's discussions.

"I don't believe you, but okay," Robin said.

"Okay, everyone, this is Brooklyn and I'm back and ready to hit you with some realness. The first question for tonight is, would you rather be wanted or needed in a relationship. Y'all want me to kick it off? I see the phones are going crazy tonight as usual. Let me start with my real, realness and then we'll go to the phone line. My realness is I would rather be wanted than needed. I want a man to want me so much that the only need he'll have is to hear me tell him how much I love him and how he makes me feel. I want him to want me to the point that his need isn't financial or tangible, but it's a passion so great that when he's not with me, he longs for when he gets to feel my body sidling up to him again. When I think of need, I think of having me around because there is something lacking that prevents him from surviving, like he can't pay his bills or clean the house or afford nice, new things. When I think of want, I'm thinking about his desire to have me in every which way possible because that closeness is what drives him to get up each day, take care of business and get back to loving me and me loving him. I once had a guy ask me if I needed a man in my life, as if my very existence was based on having a man. My response was that I didn't need one, but I desired one, I wanted one and it was all about feeling, loving, touching and being together with the goal being living our best life together. I know most people seek out a mate for how they can get their best come-up, but I've been there. You all know my story, at least the surface story. I had all that, but the love was missing. I didn't always feel wanted. I felt like I was more of a need and eventually, things turned bad because I thought that relationship could be saved, so I stuck around and tried. In the end, I got hurt and it was my own fault for settling for being a need and not a want. Going forward, I want to be wanted and I want the need to be salacious, exciting, spicy, sexy! Y'all know I keep it real on my show. I have things, I have money and what I figure is next for me is the non-tangible. It's that love so deep that I dream about it even when I'm not asleep. I want to be distracted by that kind of love all day to the point that everyone who sees me tells me that I don't even have to tell them I'm in love because they will be able to see it all over me. I want to shiver when I think of him because of the lasting affect he has on me from the last time we were together. Y'all know what I'm talking about – that good, good, good love! I want to hear from you. Tell me if you want to be wanted or needed and let's bring the real, realness!"

AND THEN THERE WAS YOU

Brooklyn looked at Robin who told her that her first caller was on the line and that it was a man named Roscoe.

"Roscoe, you're on the air with Brooklyn. Go ahead and bring the real, realness, sugar!" she exclaimed.

"Well, Brooklyn, let me put it to you like this – I love it when a woman tells me she doesn't need me, but she wants me. That's a huge turn-on for me. Too many times, we guys meet women who want to have their hands open all the time and you begin to see that's all you are to them. When a sister is bringing her own to the table, I love it because then I can focus on loving her. Now, don't get me wrong, I love spoiling my lady and I do it often, not because she needs it, but because I want to give her nice things and do nice things for her. Our relationship isn't tainted because she's sitting around waiting for my payday and wondering how much of it she's going to get. I want my lady to know I'm all about her because I want her and not because I need her. I'm not out hustling ladies who are doing big things for herself because I'm trying to get in her pockets. I want her to know our love is in my head, not in my pockets," Roscoe said proudly.

"You got them good pockets though, right? Keeping it real, no woman wants a broke man, but he doesn't have to be rich either. He needs to be handling his own. You're right, the focus can then be on the loving," Brooklyn said.

"Oh, yeah, a brother has that covered. I made sure my game was tight before I set out to make a lady fall in love with me. I own several garages and my lady and I recently went into business together to expand those garages. We're working on being that power couple and you know what, there isn't any pressure about whether I can provide. All I want her to focus on is loving me and letting me love her and building our empire together," Roscoe exclaimed confidently.

"Well, it sounds like you have one lucky lady, Roscoe. Good luck to your love. We're going to take a few more callers on this topic, but in the meantime, start thinking of your responses to what the second question of the night will be. If you had a hot next door neighbor, would you do him or would you think being right next door was too close for comfort? I want to hear from y'all on that one. I think that's really gonna set the tone for our night. Our next caller is Kimberly. Come on Kimberly and bring that real, realness," Brooklyn said and smiled when Robin gave her the thumbs up.

**

Damn! Diezel thought as he listened to Brooklyn rock yet another successful on-air show about love. He didn't know if anyone else was paying attention to her, but he heard every word she said. He listened to the comments from other listeners as well, but what stuck to him was when she gave her opinion on her second topic for the night about doing a hot next door neighbor. His mind went back to the night they met and just as he found her attractive, he could see from the way she looked him over that she was undoubtedly attracted to him, too. When she told her audience she would be open to doing her hot neighbor, but if he turned out to be more than just sexy to the eyes, but to her mind, she would want more and didn't care if he lived next door or down the street.

He also thought back to her first question of the night. He's known men who believed that a woman should need a man, but he was of the same mindset as Brooklyn and most of the callers who answered that question. He wanted a woman to want him and not just need him for what he could do for her. He'd been on the end of 'need' and it wasn't a good place to be. That made him think of his time as a married man and how hard it was because the want was purely physical and he made it more than it should have been. They went from hot desire to him being a need and it all went downhill.

He'd met Jessica five years ago at the age of twenty-six when he'd just started practicing law and right after his parents had died. Though he was focused on work, he was lost because of the hurt behind his parents' sudden death.

He and Jessica had a whirlwind affair that was all about the physical and he mistook that for love. Within one month of meeting, he'd taken her on a trip to Vegas and to the dismay of his brothers and sister, he married her. His family tried to convince him that marrying Jessica was a knee-jerk reaction and if he had been thinking clearly, he never would have married her. By the time he realized his family was right, she was already pregnant with Dani and then he tried to make it work because of her, but still it failed.

Jessica saw him as a means to her getting out of a life she hated in New York. Thankfully, Davis, the oldest of the siblings had already made sure that no one could ever touch their settlement money. He was the attorney in the family, yet he'd acted carelessly, acting out and unable to deal with his parents dying. He would have to pay Jessica child support and alimony based on his salary, but she could never get her hands on the millions he received in the accident settlement. Though a portion of his settlement had been set aside for his daughter, Dani, she wouldn't receive a monthly stipend of that money until she was twenty-five years old and by then, he hoped she'd be on her way to a good life and can handle the financial responsibility, something he was going to make sure he prepared her for. He was grateful that Davis was able to keep a level head when the rest of them were reacting while hurting.

Listening to Brooklyn reminded him what he had been missing in his relationship with Jessica and that was want. He wanted sex, but the kind of want that Brooklyn spoke of was after you know more about a person than just what they desire in bed. You want to know what they're thinking and what they're feeling so that you can do your best to be the best mate you can be. She talked about the kind of love that when two people were away from each other, the smallest remembrance of something they said or did will make you smile throughout the day. He and Jessica fought so much that it was the fighting that he focused on when they weren't together. He felt dread going home knowing the fighting would start again. It wasn't a good environment for their daughter and he knew they would all be happier if they divorced.

The separation and divorce were nasty, but it was necessary for them to finally live in peace. When he was offered a partnership in his law firm after successfully winning every single corporate law case he was given, he accepted the offer and agreed to move to the west coast. He wasn't sure he'd stay there forever, but he needed space so that Dani wouldn't have to constantly be in the middle of Jessica's wrath against him for divorcing her. He wanted to be a daily presence in his daughter's life, but even in New York, it was going to be a problem with the anger Jessica spewed at him every day.

After they separated, if he had Dani at the new condo he'd purchased, Jessica would show up day and night to see if he had women there. If he was out with someone, she would mysteriously show up with Dani in tow and cause a major disruption. She stalked him and he was again beginning to lose focus. With Dani coming to the west coast for the summer, they would have peace and time alone to really bond.

At four, Dani was his life. When he was away from her, he talked to her every single day either by phone or by facetime. Nothing was more important to him than her. He had scheduled his move to California to coincide with her not missing any time in pre-kindergarten now that the school year was over. She was coming to stay with him for the rest of the summer and he couldn't be happier, especially since they were on the beach. They not only had the ocean behind the house, but Davis also had an inground pool on the side of the house. Like his parents did for him and his siblings, he made sure that before Dani could even walk, she could swim. She loved the water as much as he did and now, she could swim every day if she wanted to. He'd already secured a camp for her and once he did a tour, he could see Dani enjoying herself and making new friends. He would make every minute of her time with him memorable.

Going back to listening to Brooklyn's sultry, seductive sounding voice, like the rest of the listeners he would be sad when the two-hour talk show portion of her show was over as the last two hours of sexy, romantic music would play with intermittent words from Brooklyn. Laying back comfortably on the beige leather sectional with Denim asleep in his lap, he continued to listen and as he did, he fell for her hard.

**

For the last two hours of her four-hour show, Brooklyn began her playlist of songs and here and there, threw in a few unexpected numbers. Knowing that she was due a thirty-minute break, she removed her headset and smiled when Robin stood and followed her out of the studio, no doubt wanting to go back to their chat before the broadcast started.

"Are you going to follow me around every time I take a break?" she asked Robin though she already knew the answer.

"I sure am. I want to know what's going on with you. Is it a new man? Only a man can have you digging deep for that really sexual side of Brooklyn I've been seeing and hearing from the past two nights. You were off the chain tonight talking about your second and third favorite parts of a man's body, talking about doing hot neighbors and let's not forget the question about multiple orgasms. It's too bad you have to be censored and can't talk about that number one part of a man that I know you love, but haven't indulged in since when now? I know it's been quite a while for you and for what reason, I don't know, but I'm curious. You've got twenty-eight minutes, so let's hear it," Robin said, opening her lunch bag and digging her teeth into the ham and cheese sandwich she'd made. "Tell me the truth. You met someone, right?" she added in between chews.

"No."

"Yes," Robin countered. "Who was it? You may not be dating him, but someone has your panties all moist and don't lie."

"You are so crass. You get on my nerves. Luckily, I enjoy your company and cherish your friendship. Like I said, I didn't meet anyone, but I did see someone and I can't remember the last time I saw a guy that good looking. He defied the description of what handsome is and then to hear him talk to his puppy like he was the most precious thing in the world had me lusting after him. He was all soft and cuddly and I was mesmerized," she said.

"Okay, who was soft and cuddly, the puppy or the man?" Robin mocked.

"Very funny. I'm talking about the man. We didn't talk for long, but there was something about him."

"Where did you meet this guy? You never go anywhere anymore."

"Right next door. He's Davis' brother, Diezel."

Robin choked on her water as her eyes glassed over while trying to catch her breath.

"Next door? Oh, so that's where the topic tonight came from? Did you just say you met a man named Diezel? Now, that's hot. If the name matches the guy, you are talking about a winner."

"You know how I'm always going crazy over the actor, Dwayne Johnson, The Rock? He looks like him in every aspect from his build to his gorgeous face."

"You've never met him before?"

"If he's been there to visit Davis, I don't think it's been in the past three years or it may have been at a time when I wasn't there. Trust me, I would not have missed seeing him."

"Mmm, he sounds hot. Did you jump him yet? You know, give that body of yours a much-needed jolt or surge? It's a good thing you aren't one of those cranky, mean women who everyone wishes would get some loving to lighten her mood up. I know what Max did to you throughout your marriage, the other women and then to find he had two children by two other women while he was married to you, but that should not have made you swear off of men."

Leave it to Robin to make her think back on her five-year marriage to Max, a time she wanted to forget about.

"Robin, I haven't sworn off of men. I've been busy with work and then promotions and appearances have really surged with the talk show. Who has time to date?" Brooklyn asked and chowed down on a few forkfuls of the salad she'd brought with her to snack on.

"Uh, hello?" Robin said pointing at herself.

"Girl, what you're doing is not dating. You're bed hopping and you know that's not me. I know my life with Max wasn't the best and in fact, it wasn't good at all, but I learned a lot about myself and what I want and that limelight wasn't it. I thought I was happy being the hot wife on his arm, which is what I was always called in the tabloids, but I am and always have been more than that. I accepted the job to do this radio show because I feel passionate about people finding their true love and not settling. People need to talk about what they've been through in order to clear a path to where they are going. I'm not an exception to that. When it's right for me, the right man will snatch me up and every day that I make him feel like he's king of the world, I'll be that queen because I'll know that I am and he'll show me that I am that to him."

Without warning, Robin clapped ceremoniously and they both laughed.

"Girl, you need to package this stuff up and write a book. I can't speak for our listeners, but I learn something every night working with you. Now, back to this hunk next door. Are you going to make a move or anything? What's up with that?" Robin asked.

Brooklyn didn't want to admit that she'd been thinking about Diezel since the night they'd met earlier in the week. He must have been busy all week because she hadn't seen him at all. She was coming into her weekend off and perhaps she'd see him during that time. She wasn't planning to do much other than relax on her deck or down on the beach.

"I'm not going to make any moves on him. You know me, I take every day one day at a time. Let me just say that I wouldn't mind sitting down and getting to know him. If he's anything like Davis, he's a great guy. Davis is like that big brother I never had and has all the qualities a woman would want in a man except for the fact that he has a problem with commitment. I don't know what it is. He's had the same girlfriend for a lot of years and he's not even thinking about marrying her and trust me, Lanie is a nice woman. We've become good friends. Lanie wants to get married and for some reason, he doesn't see the signs. I'm not saying I'm looking to marry anyone, but good guys like Davis are hard to come by and I'd hate to see Lanie finally lose patience with waiting on him."

"I like Lanie. I've met her once when I was at your house. I can't wait to meet Diezel. When are you inviting me over so that I can casually run into him and check him out?"

Brooklyn looked at her playfully, sideways.

"Never. I know you and you'll try to fix me up with him. I'm good on that front."

Brooklyn checked the time and after a few quick bites, she put her salad away.

"Time to go already?" Robin asked, finishing her sandwich.

"Not exactly, but close enough. I'm heading back to the studio. You can come when you're ready. During the next break, I want to talk about next week's show and some suggested topics to run by the program director during our roundtable tomorrow morning," Brooklyn said.

"Sounds like a plan. I'll be there in a minute."

Brooklyn nodded as she stood and walked out of the break room. Until she'd told Robin about Diezel, she hadn't thought about how much he'd been on her mind since they'd met. She definitely wanted to know more. Robin was right – she hadn't dated at all in the past few years and for the first time in a long time, she realized she was ready to do so, thanks to Diezel.

4

Sunday morning was Brooklyn's favorite day of the week because she didn't have to be on the air later that night. She loved her job, but it was exhausting pouring every bit of herself into those conversations with her listeners. Sunday morning meant she was going to spend her morning relaxing in her favorite beach chair on the beach under her umbrella either reading or listening to music. She loved doing that most Sundays and as she walked with umbrella, chair, cooler and her iPad in her hands, she was reminded that she was definitely a California girl, though she had been born and raised in Nebraska, a weird location to live even for an Armenian family. The temperatures were expected to reach into the nineties, but the water, she knew, would still be cool.

As she planted her umbrella in the sand and found the perfect spot for her chair under it, she was startled into the position of a statue when she saw Diezel jogging toward her in gym shorts, sneakers and no shirt. Goodness, she was near fainting from the sheer degree of how sexy he was.

"Good morning," Diezel said walking up to her.

"Good morning to you. I haven't seen you since that night Denim got loose. How have you been?" she asked, shielding her face from the sun with her arm.

"Getting settled in at work and working on preparations for my daughter arriving tomorrow. I'm flying out early to New York to pick her up and flying right back."

"How long is she coming for?" she asked.

"Do you mind if I sit? That way you won't have to keep your hand over your eyes to block the sun. At six-five, when standing, people still have to look up and I'm sure it's worse when they're sitting."

Brooklyn moved her chair over so that he could join her under the umbrella, out of the sun.

"Sure, have a seat," she said and patted the towel next to her for him to sit.

"You're sure I'm not interrupting anything?" he asked.

"No. I was going to sit here for a bit and then get in the water to cool off."

What she didn't say was that the minute Diezel had shown up on the beach, the sun wasn't responsible for the heat that flowed through her. She secretly hoped he didn't have a shirt nearby to put on. She loved seeing him without it.

"This is the first chance I've had to really enjoy it. Life has been a whirlwind since I moved here. I'm looking forward to a few more weeks of downtime before I have to officially start work."

"Am I prying if I ask what it is that you do?" she asked.

When she first saw him, she thought he was some kind of athlete, perhaps a football player or maybe even an actor with his strong, handsome features and extremely good looks. They were in Los Angeles, after all and hot, beefy men were a dime a dozen in the entertainment industry.

"I'm a corporate attorney, a new partner in a law firm," he stated.

Brooklyn couldn't help that her eyes traveled over him when she heard him say he was a lawyer. That was the furthest thing from her mind and she was sure she wasn't the first person to be shocked by that revelation.

"Seriously?" she questioned.

"Seriously," Diezel laughed. "Shocked right? I got it and I get that a lot."

"I love it and though I know you get that look from people, the same one I gave you, I bet you're good at it. How much do you love the house?"

"I see the pull my brother has for this place. I sat outside on the deck last night and almost slept there the whole night. The water and the quietness are exactly what I need right now and my daughter is going to love this."

"I can tell you're excited about her arrival."

"I miss her with everything in me. I'm still trying to figure out how I'm going to survive when I have to take her back to her mother at the end of the summer. I'm trying not to worry about that now, but eventually that day will come. If you hear crazy barking tomorrow, it's because Denim will get to see her after a month. He misses her, too. She has this stuffed elephant up at the house that I brought along with me and he won't let it out of his site probably because it has her smell on it."

"How old is your daughter?"

"She's four, turning five in August. I'm happy I'll get to spend her birthday with her here. I can't wait to see the look on her face when we pick Denim up from the kennel tomorrow when I get back. Every time I talk to her, the first thing she wants to know is if Denim is okay and if he misses her. After I reassure her, she then gets to how much she misses me. Imagine that – coming in second behind a puppy," he quipped.

"A girl and her puppy shall never be parted!" Brooklyn exclaimed. "You're kenneling Denim just for a few hours?" she asked.

"Yeah. I thought about taking him with me, but we'll only be a few hours."

"If you want, I can look after him. I'll be home all day tomorrow and I'd love to do it. After one encounter, I'm already attached to him."

"Really? You won't mind?" Diezel asked.

"I don't mind at all. We're already like best buddies. Bring him over before you leave and any toy he really likes. I love dogs, as I mentioned the other night. I think being around Denim will help me decide quicker to get one."

"Thank you. That's nice of you. I'm heading out around eight in the morning. Is that too early?" he asked.

"Not at all. I'm up early every day. I don't believe in wasting too much of this beautiful daylight. I like working at night, but it's the daytime that I enjoy the most."

Diezel stood. "Then I'll see you tomorrow morning. I appreciate your offer. I'm not a fan of kenneling for a short trip and Denim's not a fan either. I'll leave you to your quiet time. I'm going to take Denim out for a walk before I go check out the Santa Monica pier."

"Have fun. You're going to love the restaurants, the shops, the arcade and of course my favorite, the street performers. The Ferris wheel is everything you've ever heard about it. It's one of my favorite places to go, says the little kid that's still in me."

Diezel paused and went for it. Nothing is known unless you try, he thought.

"Would you like to join me and Denim? I found that dogs are welcomed on the pier and I think he'll get a kick out of all of the people and activity. I haven't taken him out much other than for daily walks. We would love the company and I'd like to treat you to lunch as a thank you for helping out with him tomorrow. Of course, that's if you're not busy today," Diezel said.

He'd seen the excitement on Brooklyn's face when she talked about the Pier. It would also give him a chance to get to know her and not just the very personal parts of her that she reveals to her listeners on her show.

"Are you sure? I do love going there, but I don't want to get in the way," she said.

"In the way? Not at all. I would love the company and I know Denim will enjoy having you with us."

"Then, yes, I would love to join you. What time are you going?"

Brooklyn needed him to answer quickly and walk away before she stood and did a little dance of jubilance over her excitement of spending some time with him. She didn't want to embarrass herself, but any minute, she would be unable to contain herself. She didn't know why she was inwardly acting shy because one thing she takes to her show each night is how she believes a woman should go for what she wants just as much as a man does. The rule is, there are no rules when it comes to seeing someone you like.

"I'm going to take Denim out for a walk on the beach. He loves that section that's reserved for dogs and yesterday, I think he found a little Yorkie girlfriend that tends to be there around this time. Why don't we say in an hour? Is that enough time for you to get your swim in? If not, we can say two hours? It's still pretty early."

Diezel didn't care if it was one hour or two hours, his eagerness to see her for more than just passing neighbors was off the charts.

"An hour is good. I'll get a quick swim, shower and change. Knock on the door when you're ready," she said.

"I'll do that. I'm looking forward to hanging out," Diezel said and headed toward his house.

"As am I," Brooklyn said to herself. She watched as Diezel disappeared out of sight and with no one watching, she stood and walked toward the water, adding in a little dance and smile.

**

Brooklyn was just about dressed when she heard the doorbell ring. She checked the time and didn't think it would be Diezel since only thirty minutes had passed. Perhaps he was ready earlier than he'd planned. She didn't see it as a problem as she made her way to the door after showering and changing. She only needed to do something with her hair and add a touch of make-up.

Checking the camera that was pointed right at the front door, she saw Robin and not Diezel standing there. She opened the door with a surprised look.

"Hey, Robin? What are you doing here on our day off?" she asked. "Come on in while I finish getting dressed."

"Going somewhere? You are usually relaxing when you're off for the day, yet here you are looking like you're about to head out," Robin said going into the kitchen and getting herself a bottle of water from the fridge.

"I am going out and you didn't answer my question about why you're here, not that I don't enjoy seeing you," Brooklyn said.

"I wanted to talk to you away from the station about my new contract. I received it this morning and there is a clause in it about a bonus that I would get based on an evaluation from you. I'm not sure that I understand why my bonus would be based on that. I thought it was based on my agreeing to the stipulations in the contract and staying on for another eighteen months. I was going to call you about it, but I didn't want my questioning of it to come across wrong."

Brooklyn stopped in her tracks as she headed toward the bathroom to finish her hair. The heat of the day was going to require that she wear it up to not sweat like crazy while out with Diezel.

She turned around and faced Robin.

"I don't know anything about such a clause. I was told I needed to evaluate you for a bonus, but I was told it was for the past eighteen months, not for the time of your next eighteen months. Who told you all of this?" she asked, reaching for the papers Robin was now handing her. She scanned them quickly.

"What do you think about this?" Robin asked.

Brooklyn looked at her and saw her nervousness.

"Well, for starters, you don't have anything to be nervous about. You already know you're getting a stellar review from me, so your bonus is in the bag, but that's not the point. I don't remember them asking me to ever give Curtis a rating that would impact his getting a bonus when he worked as a member on our team. In fact, I don't remember anyone else saying anything about this. I don't want to tell you what to do, but I recommend you don't sign this the way that it's worded. I should have been consulted on this before they gave you a new contract. I want you to know that I knew nothing about this, nor would I have agreed to it and it's my show."

She looked over at Robin who didn't appear to be as shook up.

"I didn't think I'd get a bad rating because you're always telling me I'm doing a great job and that we're a great team, something I appreciate. I asked a few others and no one else has that clause in their contracts and let me note that the other on-air assistants are all men."

Brooklyn huffed in frustration.

"I know and that's the first thing that crossed my mind. I'll take care of this immediately and I don't want you worrying about it. You'll get your bonus just like your male counterparts and I'm going to have this taken out of your contract. Is there anything else that seemed out of place in here?" she asked, holding the papers up.

"Just one thing. I was asked to not take off Christmas week when I typically fly to Atlanta to visit my family. That's the one week a year that we're all together and I've always taken it, asking for it early enough. I understand that one of the other guys wants that week. I'm normally off when you're off. They want me to be on hand with your stand-in that week. This guy who wants it is someone connected. I don't want to make a big deal out of it, but I don't like how that was done," she said.

Brooklyn sat in the seat across from Robin at the ten-foot bar in the kitchen.

"I'm glad you brought this to me. I have major pull around there and I'm saying not to this foolishness about the bonus and I'm also going to say no about taking away your week. I don't know what they thought they were doing not running this by me. Again, don't you worry one bit. We gals have to stick together. You're now becoming as big a part of the radio show as I am. Have you thought of having an attorney check over your contract? I always have mind read my contract over."

"I haven't, but it sounds like I should do that."

"Leave it here with me. I'll find someone to take a look at everything else in it just to be sure you're getting a fair deal."

"Thank you, Brooklyn. I don't want to be any trouble, but I felt like these things were wrong and trust me, I already knew you had no clue or you would have talked to me about them. Consider the issue dropped and I'll wait to hear from you. Now, back to where you're going," Robin said.

"Oh, right," Brooklyn said jumping up and running to the powder room to finish her hair and makeup.

"Oh, right what?"

"I'm going out with Diezel."

"What? You say that like it's a natural occurrence for you. Is this a date?"

"No, just hanging out on the Pier and enjoying the day."

"Yes!" Robin exclaimed.

"Yes, what?"

"I get to see this hottie."

Before she could respond, Brooklyn heard the doorbell and this time, she had a feeling it was Diezel.

Robin stood to go answer the door until Brooklyn stopped her.

"Don't you dare and don't ask a bunch of intrusive questions either," she playfully scolded.

"Girl, I said I wanted to see him, not get his life story. I'll wait for you to tell me that another time. Open the door," she said.

Brooklyn quickly checked herself in the mirror and headed for the door. She hadn't been this excited about going out with someone before. This was a first for her.

The minute she opened the door, she tried to remain calm, but Diezel was like a fantasy from a movie where a woman opens the door and flings herself into the arms of her handsome lover. She wouldn't go that far, but he got her imagination cranking up.

"Hi, there," she said, moving to let him in. "I'm just about ready. Hey, Denim," she smiled and rubbed his head. He playfully barked at her as she turned around.

"Great," Diezel said following her in.

"This is my friend, Robin. Robin, this is Diezel, my next door neighbor and Davis' brother. You know Davis," she said.

"I do. Is someone making men like you and Davis in a factory someplace where I can put in an order for one?" Robin exclaimed. She laughed even harder when Diezel laughed with her.

"I don't think so, but if I ever hear of one, I'll make sure to share that information with you. It's nice to meet you, Robin," he said extending his hand.

"The pleasure is all mine. Are you coming with us to the Pier?" he asked.

"No, she's not," Brooklyn hollered from the powder room.

"I guess I 'm not," Robin said. "I only stopped by to have her look at a contract that I thought was unfair.

She always has my back since I work on her team and I was right."

"Contract? Someone is trying to get over on you?" he asked.

"Sure is, but Brooklyn is going to handle them. This here is crap," Robin said holding it up and waving it around.

"Am I intruding if I took a quick look? I'm an attorney and it would be a shame if someone was trying to get over on you. You should always have any kind of contract reviewed by an attorney," he said.

Brooklyn entered the room.

Diezel turned around and looked her over from head to toe. She was beautiful in her denim jean shorts, yellow top and matching sandals.

"You look beautiful. Yellow is definitely your color, though I bet every color looks good on you," he said and winked.

"Thank you and I was just telling Robin she should have an attorney look her contract over."

"I can take a look. I don't mind helping," he said.

"Really?" Robin asked. "If that's okay with Brooklyn?" she said turning toward her.

"I don't mind at all. I'm sure Robin would appreciate it."

"Sure. I'll take it with me and give it back to Brooklyn later this evening."

"Hunky and kind. You're already the full package. Any more brothers roaming around LA I should know about and possibly meet?" Robin said jokingly, but still very serious.

"I have two other brothers, but neither live in Los Angeles. One lives in Florida and one is in New York."

"Both single?" she asked.

"Robin, this is not the dating game or an opportunity to fix your life," Brooklyn joked.

"I know, but you can't knock a girl for trying. You two have fun and thanks for checking out the contract."

"No problem. Are you ready to go to the Pier?" he asked Brooklyn.

"I am. It's going to be a great day," she said as they all walked toward the door.

"It already is," Diezel added.

5

Diezel made his way through JFK Airport excited to be picking Dani up for her summer visit with him. He'd fought hard in court for the time with her, even when he realized he didn't have to fight as hard. There was something in the way that Jessica responded that told him that she was just as excited for Dani to be coming to stay with him as he was. If he didn't know any better, he would think that Jessica was trying to get rid of Dani as if she were a burden. The only questions she had for the judge were around whether or not she would still get her checks for child support though she wouldn't have Dani for three months. Even the judge looked disappointed that the only issue for Jessica was about money. She didn't ask where they would be living, if he had secured proper daycare for her while he worked and she never asked when he would be bringing Dani back to her. She only wanted to know about money. After that was cleared up, he did ask about Dani's return date and before the judge could answer or he could request a date, Jessica blurted out the date that Dani started school and that she was fine with him bringing her back the day before that. To say he was shocked would be an understatement considering he assumed she would want some fun time with Dani before she had to go back to school. She also knows that Dani's birthday was coming up in August and she never even asked about whether she could perhaps fly to California for her birthday. It wasn't until a week ago that she realized she would have to pay for her own ticket to fly Dani out to California because the courts told them he was only responsible for Dani's ticket. She then changed her mind and told him to pick her up if he wanted her. Without haste, he made plans to do exactly that.

Rushing through the airport, Diezel looked around for any signs of his daughter and her mother and saw none. He took out his cellphone and dialed her over and over as he walked and each time, the phone rang a few times and then went to voicemail. He was glad he didn't schedule an immediate return to the west coast. Something told him there would be some kind of drama. Giving Jessica a little benefit, he thought maybe she was running late trying to pack enough clothes for Dani to take with her, which was totally unnecessary. He'd already gone out and bought her tons of summer clothes, toys and had even converted one of Davis' spare rooms into a pink and purple princess room. Dani was his life and he felt bad that things didn't work out with Jessica, but they were volatile together and his brother had been right, they were hot and heavy, but they had no connection outside of the bedroom.

He tried to do everything to smooth things over once they split. He was giving her more than the courts told him he had to give. He still didn't imagine how some women made it on what the system says they should receive. He paid for Dani to go to an expensive daycare and then private pre-school, an exclusive one that was typically hard to get into without a few years of trying to get accepted. He let her keep the brownstone they lived in as a couple and though she was responsible for paying the mortgage with the money she was already receiving from him, he still supplemented it to be sure Dani would always have a roof over her head.

Jessica had lost her drive to succeed after they met and wanted to sit back while he took care of them. Her only worry was where the next party was and how many more designer outfits and bags she could acquire. He was even more concerned when Jessica's mother contacted him after he had moved to California to ask him to think about taking Dani with him. Most days and nights, Dani was with her and not with Jessica because it seems Jessica had new friends and her mother felt that her new company wasn't good for Dani. She willingly offered to keep Dani all the time just to keep her safe and so without hesitation, Jessica left Dani with her mother all the time, sometimes for days at a time. At least he knew that Dani wouldn't miss school being with her grandmother. He didn't want to take Dani away from Jessica, but he would think about it if he discovered she wasn't doing right by their daughter.

As he dialed her again, he heard a tiny voice screaming daddy and turned around to see Dani flying toward him through the airport at a high rate of speed. The moment he saw her, he crouched down to catch her the moment she threw her little body into his arms. He couldn't wait to hold her again. He excitement grew with every step she took toward him. He had only been gone for a month, but it seemed like forever.

"Daddy, daddy!" Dani screamed as she made her way through people to get to him, dragging along a large pink stuffed animal.

As he watched for her and encouraged her on, he looked around for Jessica, but didn't see her. Instead he saw Jessica's mother walking swiftly behind Dani trying to keep up.

"Dani, slow down before you fall," she yelled.

As soon as Dani leaped in his arms, Diezel stood and plastered kisses all over her face as she giggled and squirmed in his arms.

"Oh, my goodness I have missed you! Daddy was going crazy not holding you in his arms. Did you miss me? I missed you!" he screamed and felt like he wanted to cry. He knew it would be hard to leave her when he did, but seeing her sealed how brokenhearted he was over the distance that would soon be between them when she had to come back for school.

"Daddy, you been gone a long time. I was crying for you and mommy told me I couldn't come to your house 'cause it was far away. Can I stay at your house, daddy? I promise I'll be good. I want to stay at your house all the time. Please can I stay with you? I want to stay with my daddy," Dani began to cry and he held her tighter as tears flowed down his own cheeks. He couldn't find words for the moment. Maybe he'd been wrong to move away. He was perhaps being selfish and needed to move back to New York and figure out a way to exist in the same town as Jessica without the daily grief. He held Dani out so that he could wipe the tears from her face and before he could answer her, he felt Jessica's mother's hand on his shoulder.

"I see the doubt. Don't. Don't you dare apologize for what you had to do. She's with you now and will be for the next few months. I know it tears you apart to be away from her, but think about what we talked about when I called you. This isn't the time to tell you more, but think about it and we'll talk."

Diezel nodded his head and was thankful that she was in his corner. After his own mother died and he'd married Jessica, her mother was that mother figure he'd been missing and she'd always tried to support, not just Jessica, but also him in the marriage. When they split, she tried even harder to be in his corner, especially when it came to Dani.

"Daddy is taking you to his house right now. Would you like that?" he asked and smiled when her cries subsided and she grabbed him around the neck, holding on for dear life.

"Yeah!" she screamed. "I'm going to my daddy's house, Nana!" she turned around and said.

"Yes, you are and you can stay for a while, too, until you're ready to come home for school. How is that?" she said.

"Can I go swimming daddy? Mommy never lets me. She said you don't live in the building with the pool anymore," Dani said.

Diezel knew she was talking about the condominium he lived in when he'd moved from their house into his own place in the city. Though he no longer lived in New York, he still owned the condo. He would still need a place to stay for his trips back to New York.

"Yes. You can swim every day and guess what?" he said happily.

"What, daddy?"

"My house has a pool and we will be right by a big ocean. You can get in that water, too. There are amusement park rides nearby, a zoo and Denim is waiting for you to get there!" he said lightening up what started out to be a sad moment between them.

"Yeah! Can we go right now?" she asked.

"You and daddy are going to eat and get your suit case checked in and then we're going on an airplane.

Would you like that?" he asked, setting her down on her feet. She must have thought that he was going to move away because Dani grabbed onto his leg like a lifeline. He already knew she was afraid that if she let go, he would be gone again.

"I'm hungry, daddy."

"Me, too. Let's get some burgers."

He looked and didn't see anything other than a duffle bag.

"This is all there is which is why we're late. I was waiting for Jessica to bring her more clothes and some of her favorite toys from home and she didn't show up. I waited as long as I could and I knew what time you were arriving. I didn't want you to worry."

"Where's Jessica?" he mouthed so that Dani couldn't hear.

"Atlantic City. I've had Dani since last night. She didn't tell me she was leaving. I got a text right before I packed a few things that I had for her at my house and called for a ride. Sorry," she said and looked away.

"Don't be sorry. I've bought lots of things for her to wear for the whole summer and toys galore. Don't worry about it. Smile knowing that Dani is going to be fine," he said. Diezel smiled back, but in truth, he was fiery mad inside. He would deal with Jessica another time. His only focus was on Dani.

"I knew you would. I'll take these things back with me, so that if she comes back, she'll have clothes at my house."

Diezel smiled and didn't respond to her saying "if" Dani returned. He knew what her words and the look on her face meant. Now wasn't the time to address it.

"Come give Nana a hug. You have lots and lots of fun with your daddy and make sure you call me to tell me about all the fun you're having, okay?"

Dani turned and hugged her tight.

"I love you, Nana and my daddy will let me call you, right daddy?" she said turning to look up at him.

"You can call her anytime you want and your Nana can call you all the time, too and even facetime like you do with daddy when he's not near you. I'm going to send Nana an iPad so that she can see and talk to you," he said.

"That's nice of your daddy, huh? Thank you," she mouthed.

"Daddy, I'm hungry," Dani said again.

"Right. Let's go eat. Do you want to join us for lunch before you go back home?" he asked.

"No, you go ahead and have this time with Dani. I'm going to try and reach that daughter of mine to let her know I dropped Dani off. If you need my support with what we talked about, I want you to know you have it. Dani should be with you all the time. The life my daughter is living right now is not good for Dani.

Let's talk later this summer. Have a safe flight and call me when you land," she said.

"We will and thank you for everything. I don't know where Dani would be without you," he said.

"I love you, son and never forget that. You are the best thing that ever happened to my daughter and definitely my granddaughter. Just keep doing you and I'm pleased."

"I will."

Diezel hugged her and then picked up Dani and walked away, looking back to wave as Jessica's mother walked slowly toward the exit.

"You and daddy are going to have so much fun! Are you ready?" he asked.

"I'm ready!" Dani hollered and bounced up and down in his arms as they walked.

**

Ruth exited the airport and was about to get back in the car that brought her when her cellphone rang. She answered before the ringing stopped.

"Fine time for you to be calling. I've been calling you since last night. What's going on, Jess? I expect better from you," she said.

"You always expect better and maybe one day you won't and therefore you won't be disappointed when I let you down."

"Why are you so bitter? What's going on with you with all of this partying and hanging out? You didn't even come to see Dani off for the summer. She'll be gone for three months and you didn't want to be here?" she asked.

"You're still at the airport?" Jessica asked.

"Really, Jess? Do you want to perhaps know that your daughter is safe in the arms of her father? Do you care that you never brought me the clothes and her favorite toys like you promised?"

"I'm in Atlantic City, Ma and I knew you'd take care of it. Diez didn't need clothes or toys for Dani. He's rich and can buy her whatever she wants or needs."

"That's not the point."

"Well, I'm calling now to see that he showed up, not that I didn't think he would. He's perfect Diezel, right? He never does anything wrong except marry me. Happy now that we're divorced?" she asked.

"I'm happy that he's happy and I thought you would be, too. You're free to live the party life you felt you couldn't have while being married and yet, you're still unhappy all the time. Dani deserves better. She loves you and she deserves better. She deserves a mother who cares as much for her as she does for hanging out with her friends," Ruth said as the car drove off.

"Well, he got his wish and she's with him for the summer. Maybe I'll leave her there for good since I'm a horrible mother, but then you wouldn't get to see her, would you?" Jessica said snidely.

"I love my Dani and the way you've been acting and dressing lately, dropping her off and never calling to even check on her, not returning calls from her school or attending any of the functions they have for her class. Diezel is the one who attends everything, even flying back two weeks ago to chaperone her trip to the zoo. Every month he shows up for the two days a parent is supposed to spend a day as the teacher aide. He even takes your day, knowing you're not going to show up. You are distancing yourself from being a presence in her life and it's not fair. I can't get around like I use to and if it wasn't for him, where would Dani be?" Ruth asked on the verge of tears.

"Oh, perfect Diezel. I'm sick and tired of hearing everyone's hero worship of him. He's not perfect," Jessica shouted.

"He may not be, but he's a damn good father. What about you? I love you and I'm trying to help you, but Dani is the priority here, not your hurt feelings. Maybe you should leave her with him for good."

"Bye, Ma!" Jessica curtly replied and hung up.

Ruth, disappointed at how the conversation turned out, put her phone away in her purse and turned to look out of the car window. She said her peace and smiled knowing how happy Dani was with Diezel. She would pray that her stay with him wasn't a temporary, summer visit, but a permanent one. She would miss her grandbaby, but Dani didn't ask to be born and now that she was here, she deserved the best of everything and with the way her wayward daughter was acting, the best was Diezel.

6

Brooklyn entered her house with Denim following close behind after coming back from his walk on the beach. She laughed when she remembered Diezel's comment about the little girl pup that Denim liked. When they got there, she could barely contain Denim from the little pup. She talked at length with the owner and after she left, she let Denim loose to run around while she sat on the rocks and watched him.

Her thoughts turned to Diezel and the time they'd spent the day before at Santa Monica Pier. With Denim in tow, they ended up spending the entire day there and at one point, Denim had fallen asleep and they shared carrying him until he woke up.

They walked and ate popcorn, hotdogs and other delicious foods including her favorite, ice cream sandwiches. They enjoyed playing arcade games and dancing along with the street performers and to her delight, Diezel was a great dancer. She added another check to her list of things she learned and liked about him.

Best of all, they ate at a dog-friendly restaurant, though they kept Denim in his carrier. They spent over an hour talking and the more she discovered, the more she enjoyed.

She learned a lot about his other brothers and their sister, who was the youngest. The way he remarked about her, she was an unexpected blessing that came along when their mother was in her forties and thought she was done having children. They all spoiled their sister and tried to keep her close though she often asserted her independence when she could.

Delia went college out of state and when she was home, she lived with their brother, Dalton, in Florida where he worked as a firefighter. He was the second oldest, with Davis being the oldest of all of them. Next was Dietrick who still lived and worked in New York, where the entire family was originally from. He owned a string of successful gyms throughout New York and New Jersey and she assumed they were all in great shape like Diezel.

Being the youngest boy, Diezel said he was often spoiled as Delia was and what she loved the most was how close they were. According to Diezel, they made sure they spoke to each other at least once a week considering they were spread out on both coasts. The one thing she'd missed in life was having siblings. Her parents were happy with one child and when she was young, she loved having all of their attention, but as she got older, she missed having that bond that she saw between other siblings.

While they talked, Diezel had also shared more about his journey to becoming a lawyer, taking after their father going into corporate law. He loved what he did, but more than that, he loved his little girl. He shared a little about Dani, but didn't go into detail about her mother whom she did learn he was once married to. She didn't know the specifics, but could see the weight of it on his face when he briefly talked about the time in his life when his parents were killed in an accident and he pretty much went off the deep end and did a lot of reckless things and he added to that getting married at twenty-five. Watching Diezel and listening to him talk, she could see how passionate he was about life and family, something she hadn't seen in other men she'd been involved with, especially her ex-husband.

She did share with Diezel the quick version of her own five-year marriage to a man who was over twenty years older than her when she thought she had gotten married for love, but it was because he asked after they had been dating for almost a year. He, unlike other people she told her story to, didn't seem shocked or judgmental about her marriage to a man that much older than her. He shared with her that he'd made his own mistakes and was now a better man because of it. So was she.

They talked about the things they loved to do, which for her included her nightly show. She started by telling him how she came to live next door to his brother after a divorce where she netted a pretty big sum because they had married on a whim and though he was a big-time studio executive, it was expected that he would have been more careful about making sure his money was protected. He believed he was so in love with her that he didn't have anything to worry about and back then, he hadn't landed his first billion-dollar movie. Following that movie's success during the second year of their marriage, the money poured in along with one successful movie after another for his studio. Soon Max was racing toward being worth over a hundred million dollars and one night a year before they divorced, he'd bought her the Malibu house because she always talked about them having a place to get away from it all while still living in Los Angeles. Less than a week later, she found out that he'd had not one, but two children with two other women after they were married that he'd kept secret from her. Though he apologized, she was over being that forgiving and left him.

During the divorce proceedings, the judge not only awarded her a large sum, but he gave her the house in Malibu and a condo in Miami, Florida. The large sum was because at the time when they were married, she was on the path to being a high paying model, but Max wanted her to focus only on being his beautiful trophy wife and since she was so young, he told her he would make sure she got many opportunities to make it big and have her own career and she agreed. That promise never happened and she was compensated handsomely for being arm candy, something she would never, ever be for another man again.

She had landed the radio show after receiving compliments wherever she went about how seductive her voice was. The idea for the radio show came up and at the same time, her name was tossed around. The show has thrived ever since and she has never looked back.

Her life was as perfect as it could be without the perfect man to share it with. Meeting Diezel and talking to him, she couldn't imagine any woman letting him get away.

When they got back to their homes after the day on the pier, he insisted on her going inside and locking up before he went into his own home. Once inside, he told her to flick the lights so that he knew everything was okay. It was clear to her that they were attracted to each other, something that caught her by surprise the moment she'd met him.

She had not dated much since her divorce, though there were a couple of hit or miss dates, she hadn't really clicked with anyone, but still longed to be in a loving relationship. She did, after all, host one of the hottest, sexiest radio talk shows on the air and she talked about love, sex and relationships though she wasn't in one herself. For the first time in a long while, she could see herself involved with someone. She'd been so focused on work that she never gave herself time to even think about a date or a relationship. Diezel changed all that just by being himself. She was getting the feeling that just when she thought good guys no longer existed, he comes into her life.

Looking down as she walked around her house, she smiled seeing Denim follow her every step. She pulled out the bowl Diezel had left for her and placed it on the floor before getting his food and water. The minute she filled it up, he attacked the food as if he was starving, though she knew he wasn't.

"Are you ready to see Dani?" she asked him as she rubbed his head while he ate. She smiled when he looked toward the door when she said Dani's name. She was probably seeing things, but it made her feel good to know the love he had for the little girl. Diezel mentioned he bought the dog when he lived in New York, but Dani's mother didn't want to be worried about taking care of a dog, so he took Denim to live with him. Whenever Dani came over, she and Denim would play for hours. She couldn't wait to see the reaction he'll have when Dani showed up. She was excited to meet her, too. There was no doubt that Diezel had mad love for his daughter and wondered how bad the situation had to be with her mother in order for him to move away from her. Again, she wouldn't pry, but was happy to know he would be over the moon when he had her with him for the summer. Where she thought she would have a regular ol' summer of her radio show and time on the beach, she could see it being much more than that with Diezel next door.

Now that Denim was getting his belly full, she needed to call Robin to let her know that Diezel had looked over her contract and when he dropped Denim off, he'd also brought back the contract with notes of what he would recommend she ask for a change to. According to him, her contract was pretty standard, but there were things inserted that should never be agreed upon and he put a strike through those. With Brooklyn's backing, he didn't see a reason why the network who owned the station wouldn't agree. That showed her, again, the incredible man Diezel was. He didn't have to review the contract and give feedback, helping Robin out, a woman he'd just met. He even offered to check out the new contract once it was drawn up and reminded her to let Robin know he'd do it free of charge. A friend of hers was now a friend of his, too.

"Denim, I think your poppa is winning hearts and taking names, namely mine. Who does that, huh? Who meets a woman and slays every preconceived bad notion she's ever had about men because he's what most women are hoping to find. You and Dani are lucky to have his love and affection. I hope the two of you don't mind if I yearn for a part of what him. I promise I won't try to take over, but can you put in a good word for your neighbor. Denim looked up from his bowl and barked at her. That was all the confirmation she needed.

"We're in this together, Denim," she said and went in search of her own meal. She anxiously awaited Diezel's return. She'd only known him for a short period of time and she missed his presence already.

7

Diezel drove his truck into the garage at the house, exhausted after two five-hour flights in one day. He would be this exhausted again if it meant he could see the smile that was on his daughter's face which had replaced the sad, tear-stained face he encountered at the airport.

After they had a lunch of burgers and fries in New York, they boarded and Dani slept the entire flight to California. She originally fussed when she had to sit in her own seat with the seatbelt on, but the moment the light went out, she climbed in his lap and slept until he had to put her back in her seat.

Once they landed, she woke up and he told her they were in California where he now lived. Picking up his car, he headed straight for the house so that they could both relax for the evening and she could finally get to see Denim. She talked a mile a minute about her puppy as she rode in the back, strapped into her booster seat. As soon as they pulled up to the house and he cut the car off, she asked for Denim.

"He's next door at the neighbor's house. Let's go get him and then we'll go inside and watch television because Daddy is tired from all the flying. Okay?" he asked.

Dani shook her head vigorously and happily jumped into his arms the minute he unstrapped her.

Walking next door before even going into their house, he was about to knock when the door opened up and on the other side stood Brooklyn looking like a goddess and in her arms was an excited puppy.

"Denim!" Dani screamed and squirmed down to the ground. The minute Brooklyn opened the door, Denim leaped into Dani's arms and licked her face vigorously causing her to almost fall over from laughter.

"Looks like he missed you," Brooklyn said.

Diezel stooped down to Dani's level.

"Dani, this is Miss Brooklyn. Miss Brooklyn this is my daughter Daniella, who likes that we call her Dani."

"Hi, Dani. I hope it's okay that I call you that, too even though we just met."

"Hello. Daddy she's pretty," she said.

Diezel looked up at Brooklyn from his position close to the ground.

"Yes, she absolutely is," he said keeping his eyes firmly planted on her. He'd been thinking about her the whole flight back and he couldn't wait to get back to Malibu to set his eyes on her once again.

Brooklyn blushed and due to the lightness of her skin tone, she had no doubt Diezel could see that she was.

"Thank you," she said. She wondered if he said it simply in response to his daughter, but the moment she looked in his eyes, what she saw staring back at her was honesty and confirmation that he meant it from deep down, not just on the surface. "So, I see you made it back. How was the flight?" she asked, trying to still her beating heart.

"She slept the whole flight and I napped here and there and I'm exhausted. Still, nothing makes me happier right now than having her with me," Diezel said looking down at Dani who smiled and laughed with Denim.

"Denim was the perfect house guest and for as little as he is, he sure loves to eat," she laughed.

"Something isn't it? His appetite? Thank you for helping out with him. I'm planning a day of no activity for all of us for the rest of the day today and tomorrow."

"I'm happy to meet you Dani and I know you'll have a good time with your daddy," Brooklyn said. In her head she was thinking how could anyone not have a good time with Diezel and she kept that thought in her head, at least for now.

"I love my daddy," Dani said.

"And daddy loves you. Let's go in the house so you can put Denim down and see your room. Thanks again Brooklyn. I'm right next door if you ever need anything."

Diezel turned and walked over to his house and after waving one last time at Brooklyn, they went inside.

"Is this our house?" Dani asked looking around.

"For a little while. This is uncle Davis' house. He's working someplace else and we're staying here for a little bit. Daddy has another house that's being painted and fixed up just for us. Do you want to see your room?"

"Yeah!" Dani exclaimed and ran with Denim right on her heels when he pointed her to it.

He leaned against the door frame watching her run from one thing in the room to the other. She checked out the white canopy bed with the princess trimmings, the large toy chest and started pulling toys out. What he knew she would love the most were the many books and stuffed animals on the bookshelf. When he first arrived in California, the first thing he did was have everything delivered for Dani's room and he spent the first day putting it together knowing she would be there soon. Now, the house felt like home even if it was only for a few months. He wasn't ready to think about the day he'd have to fly her back to New York and so he pushed that to the back of his mind.

"Do you like it?"

"Yes. Can Nana come see my room soon, daddy?" she asked.

"Daddy will work on that for you, okay?"

Dani shook her head, but didn't say a word as she found several books from the shelf and climbed up on the bed with them. He had his answer to how much she loved her new room.

"Can I color daddy?"

"Do you remember daddy's rule about coloring?" he asked pulling out coloring books and crayons from the chest at the foot of her bed.

"Only color on paper and coloring books, right?" she said looking up at him innocently.

"That's right. You can color while daddy makes a few phone calls. Then we're going to get you a bath and in pajamas. We're going to have sandwiches for dinner, but daddy will make you a big breakfast in the morning."

"I like our house daddy," Dani said and turned to her coloring books.

"I do, too, especially with my Dani now in it."

The look and feel of being content was unlike anything else in his life. He was now ready for life in California.

Diezel turned and walked back into the living room while he contemplated what he would say to Jessica when he reached her. Stepping out onto the deck so that Dani wouldn't hear their conversation, he dialed her phone. When she didn't answer, he left her a message, making sure to keep his tone under check.

He was furious, but there was no need to start a war. He had Dani with him and that was all that mattered.

"Jessica – I don't know what's going on or where you are, but I can't believe you didn't come see Dani off at the airport. She was going on her first flight and she's going to be gone from you for the entire summer. I expected more from you than what I've been getting lately. I'm sure Dani would like to talk to you. Call my cell anytime you want to talk to her. I hope all is well with you," he said and hung up.

Proud that he didn't let loose on her like he really wanted to, Diezel went back inside to relax. Two flights in one day is a lot for anyone, even someone like him who flew a lot. He could now exhale and enjoy the rest of the summer knowing he wouldn't have to worry about being away from Dani at least temporarily.

**

Brooklyn felt like a stalker watching Diezel pace around his deck. He was on his cellphone and whoever he was talking to, he didn't seem too happy about the conversation. He wasn't smiling and in fact, she could see that he was grimacing, a face she made when she talked to someone she had to talk to and not someone she wanted to talk to.

Turning away, she rushed to grab her phone before it stopped ringing.

"Hey, Mom!" she said overjoyed. She loved when her mother called, which was often since they lived far away.

"Hey daughter of mine. How are things in California?"

"Everything is good. I'm working hard as usual. How are things in Nebraska?" she asked.

Her parents loved their quiet life in Nebraska where her father still ran his trucking and freight company, one of the largest in the country. They traveled often, but loved going back to the quiet ranch they owned. She visited when she could which was several times a year.

"Great. Your father and I are going on a cruise next month, one of those two-week cruises. I wanted to be sure you knew in case you called looking for us and the phones were out of range. I hope you're making time for some fun and not just all work. I worry about you being in California and working around the clock."

Brooklyn laid comfortably on the sectional in her family room and talked.

"I'm trying, but you know how work can be. The show is really popular and during the day I have appearances to make for promoting the show, keeping it out there and interesting. Today, I'm finally relaxing since it's my night off. I was going to go out, but I think I'm going to hang around and enjoy being home."

"Every time I talk to you you're enjoying being at home. Don't forget there is life to be lived outside of work. I know you've done and seen a lot in your thirty years, but don't forget there is still a lot more to do and see. Are you seeing anyone yet?"

Brooklyn smiled knowing that part of the conversation would come up sooner rather than later. Every time she talked to her mother, she asked about her dating life.

After her rocky marriage at a young age and then divorce, her parents worried she would let what happened keep her from finding a meaningful relationship again.

"Not yet and I'm good. For now, I'm focusing on me and not on me with someone else."

"I know honey and that's fine. Most importantly, I want you to be happy and you know that. When I think of the drama Max took you through, you know I want to hurt him."

Brooklyn laughed out loud. "I know you do and try not to if you ever see him in person again. I'm living a good life now and despite what happened, I am very happy with where my life is. When I start dating and the right man finds me, you'll be the first to know. How's that?" she asked.

"I'll be waiting by the phone. I know how hurt you were when you found out about those new kids of his. He already had three children from his first marriage and now two babies not even a year apart? The nerve."

"He wanted more children, I guess."

There it was. That feeling of insignificance because she couldn't have her own children. She was crushed when Max stepped out and got two different women pregnant. She initially felt like she was less of a woman being unable to conceive, but then one day she realized that isn't what made her a woman, it only made her a mother and there were other ways to have children, but she would always be enough of a woman for any man.

"One day, sweetie and you know that, don't you? Your father and I will support whatever you decide to do whether it's adopt or any other option. We love you and I won't even say the word 'if' when it comes to you having children because I know you want them. When you're ready, so are we. I may even have your father find us a house in Los Angeles so that we can be close to help you out. You have more than enough support, so I don't want you ever feeling down ever again about that. You will meet a man who will love you whether you can bear him children or not. He will appreciate you for the incredible woman that you are and will want to build a life with you and plan for having children in ways other than the traditional way. I hope you're excited for that because I am."

Brooklyn loved that her mother always knew how to make her smile.

"I am, mommy. I know my self-worth isn't tied to my womb, but to my heart. When that man comes along, you are my first call."

Brooklyn thought about Diezel because a man like him is what she considered perfect.

Take care and be safe, as always. I'll call you later this week. Love you!"

"I love you, too, Mom. Tell Dad I love him and I'll talk to him soon."

Hanging up, Brooklyn thought about Diezel and walked back over toward her sliding glass door. Looking out, she didn't see him and hoped he and Dani were settling in. He looked happier when she saw him with Dani. No one could mistake the love he had for her and seeing the look on Dani's face, that love was mutual.

After talking with her mother, her mind turned to children and her desire to one have a child that looked at her lovingly like Dani looked at Diezel. There was a time when she wanted children and then discovered she was unable to bear them due to medical problems she'd had years ago. That was perhaps the reason Max ended up having children with other women. He'd already had children from his first marriage that she knew about, but she was devastated when the media revealed his secret children and her world had shattered. She wasn't sure she would ever be in love again or that a man would love her again knowing that she would be unable to bear him any children. That thought left her depressed, but today, she shook it off. This wasn't a time to think about what she didn't or couldn't have in life. Her mother was right – life was meant to be lived despite anything bad in it.

8

One week with Dani and they were settling in nicely. Diezel had a fun-filled week of him showing her all around Los Angeles, taking in the sights. It was Friday and they had just returned from the Los Angeles Zoo. Dani had fallen asleep in the car and when they returned home and she still had not woken up, he tucked her into bed and moved quietly about the house preparing for dinner and planning to look over paperwork from his job. In a little over a week, he would begin his new job and Dani would start summer camp. He was planning to do an early run to it to let Dani see that it's a nice place and she can meet the staff before being dropped off for a full day soon.

Tonight, he was planning on grilling hot dogs and burgers out on the grill on the deck, now that he'd had a lock put on the gate to the pool. He didn't want Dani or Denim having any access to it on purpose or accidentally. Going out on the deck, he placed the cushions on the chairs and uncovered the grill in preparation for when Dani woke up hungry. He was about to walk back in the house when he turned and saw Brooklyn out on her deck.

"Well, hello stranger. Haven't seen you all week. How's it going?" he asked walking over to the railing to talk without screaming.

"Hey, there! I'm good, working like crazy as usual. I've had appearances all week except for today and I'm making the best of it before I'm on the air later. How are you and Dani settling in?" she asked.

"We're good. I took her to the zoo today and she had a blast. She's taking a nap while I'm cleaning up some and I thought I'd cook out on the grill this evening. She's had a fun, yet busy day."

Diezel smiled at Brooklyn and wished he could see her more. He'd been thinking about her all week, but his main focus was Dani and getting her acclimated to California. He was also disturbed that not only did Jessica not call to talk to Dani since she'd been with him, Dani hadn't asked for her and that bothered him. She was four, about to be five and she wasn't having any kind of separation anxiety from her own mother.

A few days ago, he did get a few texts from Jessica saying she didn't need to take Dani to the airport and knew that her mother would. She also texted that she would call to talk to Dani later in the week and didn't want to intrude on his time with her. There was avoidance going on when she didn't call, but only texted.

"I'm glad she's having a good time. When do you start work?" she asked.

"I have another week of hanging out and then it's off to work and Dani goes to camp. Luckily, the camp is close to my office, so she'll be close by. I found a dog walker who is going to come through and walk Denim during the day, so I think I have everything covered. Listen, are you busy?" Diezel asked.

"No, not really. I was relaxing inside and thought I'd come out on the deck for a while."

"Great. Would you like to join us for burgers and hot dogs? It's not a whole lot, but when it comes to Dani, she's pleased with hotdogs, chicken fingers and carrots."

"Carrots?" she joked.

"Raw or cooked, she loves carrots. I make sure there are plenty on hand at all times. We'd love to have you join us and I personally would enjoy seeing you, if that's okay with you."

Diezel was going for it. He'd been next door to Brooklyn for a few weeks and he didn't want to be shy about the fact that he liked her and hoped she liked him, too.

"I'd love to. What can I bring? I have the makings for a salad that I can bring over."

"Salad sounds great."

"What time?" she asked.

"Anytime you want. We'll be here."

"Sounds good," she replied.

"Dani's still asleep and I have a nice bottle of wine we can sit back and enjoy until she's up. That work?"

"Perfect. I'll be over shortly and thanks for the invitation."

Diezel watched her start to walk back into her house and called her name. His heart fluttered when she turned back around and looked like she was turning in slow motion with her long hair blowing in the wind off of the water.

"That's an open invitation for anytime, not just today."

"I'll remember that. See you in a few minutes," she said.

Brooklyn went inside and repeated the little dance she'd done on the beach the day he asked her to join him at Santa Monica Pier. She wanted to be honest about the fact that she liked him and the invitation to his house to join him and Dani for dinner was a win for her. She headed straight for her kitchen and began pulling out all of the ingredients to make a salad.

**

Diezel checked on Dani who was still sleeping as he looked around to be sure the house was tidy. He didn't have to worry about Denim who was laying at the foot of her bed napping along with her. Closing the bedroom door, he was excited about Brooklyn coming over and he didn't want her to think he lived as a slob. The only things he saw laying around were Dani's books and toys and he left them where they were since they were out of the way. While he waited, he remembered he needed to call Delia back. She had called while they were at the zoo and his cellphone had been in the truck while they walked around. He dialed her number and waited through three rings, thinking he would get her voicemail when she answered.

"Hey, sis!" he said with excitement. He missed Delia and hated that he didn't see her more often. In age, he was the closest to her and never wanted to be too busy to check in on her.

"Diez! Took you long enough to call your only sister back. You only have one and you ignore me for hours. Shame on you," she quipped.

"Funny. I was out and my phone was in the truck. What's up? You said your call was important," he said.

"It was and still is. I've been calling your crazy ex-wife so that I could talk to my niece and she hasn't answered or returned my calls. You know I'm two seconds from flying to New York and tapping that...."

"Don't say it and you need to stop. You and Jessica are like oil and water."

"Oh, so you mean a lot like you and her were then, right?" she joked.

"More jokes. Okay, I'll give you that."

"Seriously, what's up with that? I'm not trying to have to deal with her ignoring me when I want to talk to my Dani. She's so wretched."

Though he knew Delia was joking, she was serious at the same time. He was the only of their siblings that had a child, though his brothers were all older than him. Each were too busy chasing their dreams to settle down, claiming bachelorhood as a lifestyle. He hated that his family had to go through Jessica's drama to connect with Dani. Knowing how crazy life could get for him, he appreciated that his siblings all tried to step in when they could.

"Calm down and don't worry about it."

"I want to talk to and see my niece. I was hoping to fly in next week to spend a week at your condo there and see if she would let me have Dani for the week. Being away at school, I never get to see her and now I can't seem to reach Jessica to even talk to her. That's fowl and you know it. I know she's getting all of my messages."

He could hear her frustration and hopefully he could get another word in to explain.

"Dee, if you'll calm down for a minute, I can explain. Dani isn't in New York with Jessica. She's here in Los Angeles with me. I picked her up last week for the summer."

"Really!" she shouted.

Diezel had to pull the phone away from his ear.

"Seriously, Dee. Could you scream any louder? I don't need to hear out of this ear. Yes, she's here with me. I didn't have a chance to tell anyone other than Davis that the judge ruled that I get the full summer each year."

"Well, let me talk to her. You let me go on and on knowing she was there. You love torturing me."

"I wasn't torturing you. I was waiting for a chance to get a word in to explain and finally I took a leap and put it out there. You can't talk to her right now because she's asleep, but the minute she's up, I'll call you so you can facetime with her. That work for you?" he asked and already knew the answer.

"You already know, so don't even ask me a crazy question like that. I miss my baby and I know she misses me. How did Jessica handle having to turn Dani over for the entire summer?" she asked.

"You want the truth or do you want the story I was thinking of making up to make her look like a better mother than she has been lately?"

Diezel tried to have an open mind but couldn't figure out what was going on with Jessica. He gave her anything she wanted when it came to Dani and tried to keep the peace and yet, she was still being troublesome.

"I want the truth," she said.

"Okay, she was originally supposed to bring Dani to me and I would pay for Dani's flight. When she realized she had to pay for her own flight, she changed her mind and demanded that I fly to New York to pick her up. I didn't question it. I booked a flight and went to pick my baby up. She didn't even bring her to the airport, her mother did. Jessica was in Atlantic City partying. She still hasn't called to talk to her since she's been here and the weird part is, Dani hasn't asked for her either."

"That is strange. I talked to Dietrick and he said whenever he spent time with Dani since he's the only one of us still in New York, Dani cried whenever he took her back home."

"I don't know what's going on, but I will talk to Jessica about it whenever she decides to return my calls. Right now, she's only texting. I'm letting it go for now because my time is all about Dani and not about Jessica."

"Okay, then I'll fly to California instead of into New York to see her. You staying at Davis' house still?" she asked.

"Yes, I am. My house will be ready in about six months. I'm having a lot of work done."

"I hope that includes a room for me since none of you will let me have my own house."

"Dee, you are not ready for your own house. Dalton told us when he comes home after his shifts at the station that the house is a mess. You have your apartment at school and that's good for now. You're moving into a larger one for your last year in the fall, so stop complaining. Yes, I have a room for you at the house as we all do. Home for you is all of our houses. When are you coming here? I start work next week and Dani will be in camp."

"Camp? She can hang out with me during the day."

"Not gonna happen. I want her in camp around a lot of other children and not hanging out being a beach bum with you all week. She'll be excited to see you and so will I."

"I think I'll come next Sunday. Did you and Davis talk yet?" she asked.

Diezel smiled and could imagine Delia was probably biting her bottom lip, easing into the conversation about her moving to the west coast permanently after graduation. She was pursuing a career as an actress and there was no better place for her to be than in Los Angeles near Hollywood.

"We did, sort of."

"What did he tell you?" she asked.

"You know what he told me."

Delia huffed at him on the phone.

"Come on, Diez. I want to know if he told you the full story to help plead my case," she said.

"He told me everything about you wanting to move here after graduation next year, which I think is fine. I still think you should live with one of us at least the first year. I'm not comfortable with you being out on your own here. It's not the same as where you go to school. This is the real big, rich town and you know we worry about you."

"I told Davis I was fine with that and I also told him I wanted to live with you which was also his preference. He was concerned he would be gone a lot, which would be fine, but since you're both living there, the best choice would be with you. Now, that I know you have a room for me at your house, I'm all for that. What do you think?"

Diezel waited to respond, knowing he was testing her patience. She was the least patient of the entire crew. When he heard her sucking her tongue on the other end, he knew he'd kept her waiting long enough.

"That's fine with me. We can talk about the specifics when you get here. Your main focus is still on graduating next spring. You know we're all proud of you."

"I know and after the trouble I put you all through back when mom and dad died, I'm far past who that wild child was. Listen, I wasn't doing much this summer here in Florida. I was thinking of taking some acting classes I found out about on line, but what if I stayed the rest of the summer with you and helped with Dani? I can find better classes there, I'm sure and I would get more time with Dani than just a week or two."

"You know you're always welcomed to stay with any of us at any time. There is plenty of room here at the house for you and this is the land of opportunity for a career in entertainment. Let Dalton know and text us all your flight information. How's the credit card balance?" he asked.

Each of the brothers took turns paying her bills, but he monitored her spending more than the rest.

"It's good. Dalton paid the last bill and the balance is at zero. I haven't overspent since my trip to Cabo last year. Proud of me?" she asked.

Diezel laughed at her lazy attempt at garnering

sympathy.

"Good and don't change that when you get here."

"But, it's California. I'm suppose to shop and when in Rome...you know how the saying goes."

"We'll talk about that later, too. Call with flight arrangements and I'll pick you up from the airport."

"I will," she answered.

Diezel turned when the doorbell rang. He smiled knowing it was probably Brooklyn.

"I know school is a priority. I'll be in the acting mecca of the world. I still plan to go to graduate school and can find a good school for that there."

"Alright, sis. I have to jet. I have company at the door. I love you," he said.

"Wait company? Is it a woman? You've been out there a few weeks and you're already knee-deep in some woman? Who is she?"

Diezel laughed with familiarity at her berating him.

"I would answer that, but I don't want to. I'll see you next Sunday," he said walking to the door.

"Diez – really?"

"Bye, Dee. Now, say you love me and hang up because you ain't got nothing coming by way of information."

"Diez? Come on!"

"Say it, Dee," he pushed.

"I love you, big brother," she finally said.

"I love you, too. See you next week."

Hanging up, he opened the front door and

everything in him brightened. On the other side stood Brooklyn looking like every beautiful vision in every dream he's ever had.

"Hi," he said and moved so that she could enter.

"Hello to you. I come with salad in hand," she said. "I'll put it in the kitchen. Is Dani still sleeping?" she asked.

"She and Denim are. He doesn't let her far out of his sight. He's at the foot of her bed. I'll give her another hour and then I'll wake her up so that she'll sleep the full night. Would you like some wine?" he asked following her into the kitchen.

"I'd love a glass."

"Good. Why don't you go have a seat out on the deck and I'll join you?"

"Thank you. You know, it's refreshing meeting and knowing you. You are a one of a kind guy and I like you," she said and meant it.

"I'm glad because I like you, too. I hope that's evident."

"Well, if it wasn't, it is now and I'm glad. I'll meet you out on the deck."

Diezel smiled as he watched her walk out. Grabbing glasses and the bottle, he walked in the direction that could possibly lead to his destiny.

9

Forty-five minutes of conversation and Diezel was blown away by the woman who sat opposite him as they enjoyed a glass of wine out on the deck. No one could have prepared him for meeting the woman next door and falling for her almost immediately. He could say he was attracted to her before he met her, like many who probably listened to her reveal her innermost thoughts on the air, but it was more than that.

Brooklyn shared a lot about herself that wasn't told when she shared during her radio broadcast.

She told him about the turmoil she'd gone through being married to Max Decker, a man who was now worth millions. From her words, she had been broken after their split, but slowly came back into the woman she was always meant to be. Like him, she loved deeply and wanted the same in return, but that didn't happen. She'd met Max when she was barely twenty-one while he was much older. She was fascinated with him and was about to embark on a stellar career as a model, something that never panned out for her.

She'd struggled to find herself again and was now in a happy space. Hearing that made him happy for her.

Brooklyn loved her family; her mom and dad and she went home to visit them as often as she could. They were getting to know each other and everything he heard, had him liking her more and more.

"You know, I listen to your show most nights," he said.

"You do? What do you think?"

"I think your show gets people talking and sharing honestly about topics they probably would not otherwise share. I've thought of calling in a time or two and a few attempts I made, I couldn't get through. Your lines are always busy with people trying to get through."

"Really? What were the topics you tried to call in on?" Brooklyn asked. She liked knowing that he was interested enough to listen to her two-hour broadcast which was saying something considering it didn't start until midnight.

"One topic was on whether men prefer women who take an aggressive role or submissive role in the bedroom. That was a steamy subject and I had my own thoughts about that," he admitted and locked eyes with Brooklyn to let her know that he wasn't one to shy away from any conversation.

"I know we aren't on my show, but what are your thoughts on that?" she asked nervously.

Brooklyn would love any opportunity hear his thoughts. Her interest in him was getting deeper and deeper by the day. If they could talk about topics like what her show offered and do so comfortably, that was yet another check in her book when it came to him.

Sitting his wine glass down on the table, he looked her in the eyes.

"As for me, I like a woman who is both aggressive and submissive depending on the vibe. Some men like to always be in charge and prefer their women to submit to whatever direction he sets, but I'm not like that. If I'm with a woman and she knows what she wants and how she wants it, I want to know about it. If she wants to push me back on the bed and have her way, I'm going to lay back and let her go for hers because her satisfaction is more important than mine and it's always that way. On the other hand, if a woman wants to lay back and be loved and worshipped as the queen she is, then I'm all for showing her what he means to me and how much I desire her. I love intimacy with a woman and when we're in the moment, she knows my focus is on her and only her. The moment can be erotic whether she's taking the lead or whether I am. It's always about communication and each person getting what they need, however they need it. If they are truly in sync, there shouldn't be any problems when it comes to intimacy."

Brooklyn started to respond, but found it hard to find words. Her mind was all over the place seeing Diezel as the aggressive one taking the lead and pleasing her every way possible known to man and she could also see herself getting acquainted with every part of his body from head to toe and not just with her hands – she was thinking about the mountainous regions of his body her tongue could explore. Her mouth went dry, yet there was a part of her that suddenly moistened.

"Wow," she finally said after taking two sips of her wine to saturate her dry mouth.

"Wow? That's it?" he laughed.

"I'm trying to find more, but the visual took over and I couldn't think straight. You don't hold anything back, do you?"

"You have the intimate talk show at night. You keep it real and so do I. I'm not shy about anything and you don't know if you don't ask or if you don't share. I'm an open book."

"I like that and it's damn right sexy," Brooklyn said and then fanned herself.

Diezel laughed a hearty laugh, tossing his head back as he did so.

"I'm open about my love for a beautiful woman and nothing gives me more pleasure than to pleasure her or to let her know how much I want to pleasure her."

Making his point, Diezel looked Brooklyn over from head to toe and without thinking, he licked his lips like he'd just sampled something delicious. To him, he just did, but only with his eyes.

"My goodness. You didn't just do that," Brooklyn said breathlessly while her eyes focus pointedly on his gorgeous lips, now coated with a thin sheen. She was losing control and her body was leading the way.

"Sorry, I have a terrible habit of licking my lips. You don know that you are exquisitely beautiful? Any man in his right mind and sight can't miss how sexy you are. I'm not immune to that and it's not the wine talking. I've only had a chance to take one sip. I'm in full Diezel mode when I'm encountering a gorgeous woman. You, Brooklyn, are even more than that."

"I wish I could say you were giving me lines, but I can read your eyes and you're serious," she said, gulping when more words got stuck in her throat.

"Any more questions? Anything else you'd like to know? When it comes to my love for women, I'm always this open," he admitted.

"I have no doubt you have no issues in the woman department. I can't even imagine that ever being a problem," she said.

"I admit that I've spent more time in beds for the sake of satisfaction only, but that's not the kind of life I want. I would love to find a woman that I could commit to, love and build a wonderful relationship with. I went through a lot the past few years and after that, the only thing that I could indulge in is women who understood that sex with me didn't equate to anything long-term. It was all about the mutual gratification and I don't find anything wrong with that."

"I understand that and after you told me about your parents and the accident and how your wild days after that were now behind you, I know that you struggled to find your footing again."

"If I didn't have Dani, I don't know if I would have found my road to the right direction. She set me back to being focused because I wanted the best for her and at one time for her mother when I was married to her. I woke up and I don't mean in the literal sense of the word. I did though, and I realized I was holding her and I back from a happy life. I then found happiness in one woman after another and that wasn't the answer either. Life was spiraling out of control, but the whole time, the only real foundation I had was my work as a lawyer. I was focused on that and thrived in that, but personally, I was losing my grip, which is why I ended up out here. Leaving Dani was the hardest thing I ever had to do, but what she was witnessing between her mother and me wasn't good for her. We were too close in proximity and Jessica could be outrageous when she was angry. I trusted the decision to move here when I was offered partnership in the firm, something not offered to attorneys my age. When I was told I could pick the location, I chose this one because my brother was out here and it was far enough away that I could rebuild my life in a drama free zone. My finances would allow me to get to my daughter whenever I wanted to and so I thought it was a good move," he said.

"Then there's Dani, right?" she asked. Brooklyn knew he had to be hurting when it came to missing out on parts of Dani's life being in California.

"Yes, and then there's my baby girl. Until a month or so ago, I was in New York and then I was gone and though I talked to her every day or facetime every day, it wasn't the same. I didn't realize how bad it was until the day I picked her up at the airport. She cried because she missed me and wanted to see me and couldn't. Uh, that hurt me to my core. It's made me rethink my decision to move. I never, ever want my daughter to think I'm not there for her, but that's something I will have to deal with at the end of the summer. For now, I want to be sure she understands how much I love her. I intend to make the most of this summer. Can I be honest about something else?" he asked and turned so that his body faced hers. When she put her wine glass down and turned to face him, he gave it to her straight, no chaser.

"Sure," Brooklyn said.

"I like you and I like you a lot. I know we've only known each other a few weeks, but I like what I know about you. You're more than Brooklyn Hunter, radio personality. That woman is just as fine as the laid back, chillin' Brooklyn Hunter I'm encountering now and I'm enjoying all facets of you. I'd like to take you out on a real date, but of course I have Dani and I don't know anyone to trust to leave her with for a date night out, but I wanted you to know if I did, I would ask you out for dinner or something in a hot minute. I'm not just saying this to get you in bed, but because I truly enjoy your company and I hope that it's not just me out on this cliff alone in how much I like you," he admitted and waited for her response.

When Brooklyn reached over and took one of his hands into both of hers, he looked down at where their hands were joined and then back up to her eyes. He hadn't noticed the light specks of gold that flashed in her light-brown eyes. She was so beautiful that he was actually experiencing a woman taking his breath away.

"I like you, too, Diezel and that's not just because you said that to me. The moment you opened that door the first day, I felt drawn to you and with each time that we've been able to talk and get to know each other, I find myself being attracted to more than just the physical that is you and you already know how fine that is," she joked.

"I told Davis I had met you and scolded him for not telling me he had a neighbor as fine as you and then to find that said neighbor was Brooklyn Hunter. Don't think I'm star struck. To know how genuine and down to earth you are, I was hooked."

"Well, don't let the fact that you have Dani keep us from going out on a date. I have no problem going out on a date with you with Dani and Denim in tow. I know you're a packaged deal and I like and respect that. A perfect night is like tonight, sitting out here talking, enjoying a glass of this good wine and soon cooking hotdogs and burgers on the grill with you and your daughter. I don't need much when it comes to dating. You and I are both pretty well off and so money is not an issue when it comes to being impressed or being guarded. We each have our own which leaves us with really getting to know each other. I want that if you do," she said.

Diezel searched for the words to say, but his eyes drifted from the intoxicating pull of her eyes to the heady magnetism of her full lips, lips he'd been thinking about kissing from the first moment, not when she arrived for dinner, but the day he first encountered her standing on the other side of his door holding Denim in her arms. His heart raced erratically when her eyes shifted from his eyes to his lips the way his eyes had just caressed hers. They were thinking the same thing, but neither said it.

Taking a chance that the desirous look he saw in her eyes meant she longed for a closer connection than sitting and talking, he learned forward and in a quick motion, he tilted his head and with eyes open to not miss a single minute of her reaction to him, he caressed her lips with his, first the upper and then the lower. Without warning, an electric jolt snapped through him as a feeling of awareness and penetrating desire overwhelmed him. Pressing against her lips, he kissed her passionately until her lips opened for him and he took that moment to delve further into her mouth, going deeper, penetrating any barrier of doubt either of them had about their attraction to each other.

As their heads moved back and forth, trying to get even closer to each other, Diezel leaned his body forward, still connected with Brooklyn in a pervading lip-lock that neither wanted to release the other from and pulling her body closer to his, he stood bringing her with him. When he stood to his full height, lifted Brooklyn into his arms and wrapped her legs around his waist. The moment her arms encircled his neck, the only sounds heard were their moans and groans and the extra loud pounding of his heart.

Diezel reached around and pulled her body flush against his, gripping her plush behind in his hands as he molded her body to the fit of him. He didn't care that she would be able to feel the massive hard-on that grew longer and harder the longer he held her in his arms because he wanted her to know how much he wanted her.

Breaking the kiss, he leaned back at the same time as Brooklyn and both appeared to be working hard to still their stressed breathing.

"My goodness, that was some kiss," she said.

"You feel amazing in my arms," Diezel uttered through breaths he was still trying to catch and control.

Brooklyn looked down to where their bodies were connected.

"Am I being too forward if I say you feel amazing to me?"

To bring her point home, Brooklyn moved her hips a little and feeling him rise even more, she moaned again and this time, kissed him more intensely than they had just been kissing. She felt like a mad-woman, never wanting to let go of his lips, delighting in how her body zinged with desire she'd missed.

"Okay, now, that was just crazy. What the hell kind of kiss was that? I feel like going inside and writing you a check for that in any amount you want," he joked.

"I have a black card you can have," Brooklyn laughed, adding to the humor of the moment.

"All my avoiding women lately thinking I would never desire anyone as much as I desire you right now, yet here I am trying to find the words that would explain why I don't want to set you back down on your feet."

Brooklyn wrapped her arms tighter around his neck, using one hand to caress the nape of his neck.

"It's because you and I are feeling the same thing. I don't know where that moment came from, but it wasn't enough was it? One second we were talking about getting to know each other more and all I can think about is getting naked."

Diezel laughed, not because her comment was that funny, but because she was all in his head, reading his mind.

"That went fast and though I've thought about kissing you, I had no idea it would deliver a wallop of a punch to my gut like it did. That kiss was amazing. I think I could feel it in my toes," Diezel laughed.

"Your toes? Haha, now that's really funny. That was a powerful connection."

Diezel leaned forward and kissed her again. "There is a lot more. Before I forget that I'm a gentleman and move to the next level, I'm going to go get Dani up from her nap and start working on dinner. I need a cold shower or something. I meant it when I said I wanted to get to know you and the last thing I want to do is rush to end up where I always end up, in bed. Not that I think that's a bad place to be with you, I get the feeling if I take my time, the more I'll get to know about you will be well worth it. I'm really interested in you, Brooklyn," he admitted.

Diezel had never admitted that he wanted more from a woman than the physical, not even with his ex-wife. With Brooklyn, he didn't want to be casual. He'd done that enough over the years and now he was looking for something more. What that more was he wasn't sure, but Brooklyn wasn't a temporary fix for his horny state of mind and body. He didn't just want sex, he wanted to make love to her. He didn't want just the physical, he wanted the whole package that involved dates, feelings and more passion than even his mind and body could stand.

Before he lost his will-power all together, Diezel put Brooklyn down and then adjusted himself inside of his slacks. This moment was definitely taking every bit of strength in him.

"I'm with you and for a few moments, I almost forgot myself and was seriously ready to jump you. I like you too much to do that when I think there's something deeper that can be had here. I struggled for a long time with date after date and nothing really panning out. I haven't felt any kind of real connection with anyone in a long time and then there was you. There you were standing in that doorway looking like a woman's prince charming and little did I know, I would find you irresistible on a level that wasn't just physical. Back to our conversation, yes, I want to get to know you, too. I told you what that visual of your response to my radio show question had my mind going to and I need to replace that with a less spicy rated image. You get Dani and I'll help get things set up. Do you mind if I rummage around in the cabinets for plates and utensils? I want to help," she taking a step back from him, knowing if she didn't, she may leap back into his arms and then all bets would be off.

"Sure, but first, one last kiss that will tie me over for the night."

This time, he saw Brooklyn lean into him and when she took control with zeal, he knew that he'd just experienced her submissive and aggressive sides and he looked forward to enjoying both.

10

Diesel walked out of the front door of the house to head next door to get Brooklyn for their first official date. Delia had finally flown into California a week ago and with her help, he and Brooklyn were spending quiet time together.

Before Delia arrived, they had gone on dates and had taken Dani with them every time they went out. He loved his daughter, but he was looking forward to a meal where they couldn't use their fingers to eat. The biggest plus was with Dani around, he had full control over his libido when it came to how turned on he always seemed to be in Brooklyn's presence. She did it for him and his body reminded him of it every time, except when his daughter was around. He wouldn't have her around to save him tonight. His desire for Brooklyn was on a level he'd never had for another woman. It wasn't just her outer gorgeousness that drew him in because she was a full package with everything he loved in a woman all wrapped up in one beautiful package. He hoped to one day unwrap her like she was his favorite Christmas gift under the tree. Though they loved having Dani along with them on dates because with her there was never a dull moment or a moment of not talking about her favorite Disney characters, and they will again, but tonight was a grownup night with grown up drinks and he wouldn't have to break apart chicken strips or cut up hotdogs.

For the week since they had practically devoured each other on his deck, they had played it cool. He spent time indulged in work and Dani and she'd had several appearances to promote her late-night show. There was even talk of taking her show to television, something he looked forward to being able to celebrate with her for if it came to pass. He kept his fingers crossed that it would pan out. The little time they were able to spend together, the went for car rides and spent a lot of time talking on the phone even though they were right next door and could have visited each other. Instead, they went the old-fashioned route of Diezel courting her and he thought it was appropriate to go a route that didn't involve them hitting the sheets.

Just as he was about to knock on her door, it opened and his ability to control his body's reaction to Brooklyn disappeared. She opened the door further and locked the main door behind her before turning around and giving him a full view where his only thought was that he was in trouble. His plan of taking things slow was peeling away one layer at a time and speaking of layers...he was imaging all of hers being stripped away, starting with the body hugging, short white mini dress she had on. Her body was definitely made for it, his mind said as he willed his lips to not express what he was really thinking.

"Okay, you're not playing fair. Our first date out alone and I'm going to spend it foaming at the mouth because of you in this dress."

Diezel took her hand and held it in the air while he watched her take a slow spin. When he whistled, she laughed out loud.

"I'm glad you like it. You'll have to thank my parents for what you see. My Armenian heritage has a long line of shapely women and though I love to work out, I give credit to good genes," she said.

"Like is an understatement to what I'm thinking and as much as I would love to thank your mom and dad, I'd be too ashamed of my scandalous thoughts when it comes to what I feel when I look at you like I am right now. You look amazing and I promise to keep my foaming to a minimum as much as possible," he said taking her hand and walking toward his car parked in front of the garage.

"You look incredible yourself. We're going to be the best dressed couple wherever we go tonight. In fact, where are we going?" she asked as he helped her into the car.

Diesel raced around, got in and started the car up. Before pulling off, he turned toward her. He tried to hold back, but he needed a little something to relax him because he was a second off of turning the car off and going inside of her house with her instead of going to dinner. He needed something to douse the raging fire sizzling through his loins. His body was burning out of control with desire and he wasn't sure he'd be able to sit through dinner without constantly adjusting himself, moving what he knew would be a persistent hardon to a less visible state.

"I'm sorry," he said.

Brooklyn turned toward him and didn't know what happened that he needed to apologize.

"You're sorry? For what? What happened? Did you forget something and we're not going to dinner?" she asked.

Brooklyn was on the verge of being disappointed. She had been looking forward to their date all day, even spending over an hour getting all the important parts waxed, just in case.

"No, we're still going. I'm apologizing for messing up your lipstick," he admitted.

Brooklyn reached for the visor to check her lipstick in the mirror.

"What? There's nothing wrong with it," she said smiling at him.

Diezel smiled a devilish grin.

"Right, not yet," he said.

His gazed zeroed in on her luscious lips, covered in pink lipstick and shining, no doubt, from the gloss she added on top. He could only think of how soft they would feel and how sweet they would taste. He didn't want to wait any longer to find out.

Before either of them could say another word, he reached across the car and lightly pulled her chin toward his face and kissed her, not caring that he was going to be wearing her lipstick. He hoped she'd brought it with her to reapply it. He felt like he couldn't breathe until he had a taste of her and no matter how he tried to reason with himself, he still didn't understand how he got so lucky to be out on a date with her.

When he originally went in for the kiss, he was planning on something light and sweet until later, but that is far from what happened.

As their lips mated and their tongues swirled around each other inside of Brooklyn's mouth, his mind was spinning as he moaned, loving that she was giving as much as she was taking. As their mouths dueled intimately, he felt her soft hand on his face encouraging him on as an overwhelming need to oblige settled over him. When they finally separated, he smiled as his gaze again landed on her lips, looking a little fuller after being thoroughly kissed by him.

"Again, let me say I'm sorry," he said.

Brooklyn couldn't resist rubbing her manicured nails across her own lips, caressing the spot where his lips had just been. The feelings he left her with were powerful and if she ever needed an example of what it felt like to be intimately compatible with a man, Diezel was it. She could only imagine their chemistry in bed.

"For that kiss, you should never apologize and I have more lipstick."

"That's a good thing because I have a feeling I'm going to mess it up again," Diezel teased.

Brooklyn pulled the stick of her favorite Fenty Beauty Starlit Hyper-Glitz Lipstick in her favorite shade, Supanova and gloss from her bag and waved them at him.

"I have as much lipstick as I'll need and if you happen to have more kisses than I have lipstick, I know where to get more," she smiled sexily letting him know that she accepted the challenge. Grabbing a tissue from the small pack in her purse, she used it to wipe remnants of her lipstick from his lips.

"Thank you," he said backing out into the road.

"I wouldn't want everyone to know what we were doing or how addicted I already am to being kissed by you," she laughed. "Where are we going for dinner?" she asked as she applied her lipstick.

"That feeling is mutual, sweetheart. We're going to the Sunset Restaurant right here in Malibu. I checked with Davis and it's one of his favorite places to eat when he's home. According to him, they know him by name. Besides good food, there's a dynamic view of the ocean. I secured his favorite table with the perfect view," he said.

"I've never been there. I'm excited."

As they drove along, they talked until he pulled up

at the restaurant which was a few miles down Pacific Coast Highway, not far from where they lived. Once he parked, Diezel came around to help her out.

"I'm telling you this dress is going to be the death of me tonight," he said as they walked.

"Make sure you don't die until after I take you back to my place and have my way with you. If you're going to check out tonight, I don't want it to be before I find out what I would be missing out on if you do," Brooklyn teased.

Diezel almost choked on his next words as he coughed through her bluntness which caught him off guard by the sight of her doing so.

He leaned his head back and chuckled from deep within his chest.

"Where have you been all my life?" he leaned down and whispered in her ear as they were escorted to their seats.

"Make sure you hang around and find out," Brooklyn said as she sat.

After the waiter brought their menus and took their drink orders, they settled in to talk.

"Tell me how you ended up doing the talk show. I have listened off and on over the past two years and I love it. You get personal with your listeners, sharing your own stories of good and bad when it comes to love and relationships. I'm not sure I'd be that open," he said.

"I know I've told you some about my life of being

married to Max. Let me go a little bit deeper. Eight years ago when I was twenty-two, I married Max after what was a whirlwind affair and I was caught up in how successful he was as a movie studio executive and also for what I thought he could do for the career I wanted as a model. I was young, I had big dreams, saw money and all the promises he made me when it came to stardom and none of it happened. I wasn't happy, never became a model because he wanted me as the trophy wife and I put up with years of infidelity on his part. I woke up one day and decided to leave it all behind and find me. I remembered the self-worth my parents had instilled in me that I had temporarily forgotten for years and I got back to being Brooklyn. The one thing that kept me focused back then was the fashion column I wrote for on a monthly basis and women would ask me questions about being sexy and how to work what they had behind closed doors in the sexiest attire possible. I'm a fashion fanatic and it was crazy that so many young women looked to me for advice. After the divorce, there came another love for blogging and that became so popular that one day I was asked if I ever thought about doing a live radio show on relationships since I was doing that in my blogs. All my life, I've been complimented on the sound of my voice by men and women alike, so I figured, why not? The show took off from the very first one and I've been in love with doing it ever since," Brooklyn explained.

"So, people saw you as an expert on love and sex from the advice you gave?" Diesel asked.

Brooklyn was about to answer when the waitress stepped up to take their orders. After being alone again, she gave him more of her truth.

"I think it was more of them hearing someone come to them with truth and honesty when it comes to love and sex and how I keep it real. It certainly wasn't due to my background in being successful in love because my own messed up life was no example when it came to love. I didn't just talk about the good that I knew about sex and relationships, but I talked about my fears of not being good enough or sexy enough, despite people always telling me I'm beautiful. Women hear those words a lot, but they have to know it for themselves before it will really sink in. I talked about what people would think about topics, but weren't comfortable saying out loud until they called in to my show. At first, I was hesitant about sharing because even though I had a rough marriage with Max, I didn't want to put him out there as a villain. One day he called and told me that he was a villain and was sorry for what he'd done to me. It didn't take away the pain of the sting of my personal life being fodder for the media and he told me that he had no problem with me sharing what I'd been through because he could handle it. He wanted me to find my happy and he could tell the show was that. After that, I really got personal and the show really thrived."

Diezel shook his head in agreement. He could hear her love for what she did in every one of her shows. He had never met a woman before who was so self-aware, self-assured and valued her self-worth like Brooklyn did. Not just from her shows, but from what he'd learned about her since the moment they met.

"I can tell you love it and I love listening to you at nights. I could be creepy and say it's all the sex talk that I like, but that's not it. It's how open and honest you are about what you like in a relationship in and out of the bedroom. It's about your truth about the lessons you've learned and how you tell them there is no manual in being in a relationship or being in love. You tell them to write their own stories of love based on what they want from their mate, what they want to bring to the table and where they want things to go. When they are open about that and truthful with their mate about their own desires, they are going into a situation with the cards on the table," Diezel said.

Brooklyn acknowledged her agreement with a smile. "Very true. Tell me, what is it that we're doing? Hanging out, friends and neighbors, looking to be lovers, more than that? Are we dancing around a casual fling because of the close proximity of where we live or something more? I know we both feel the attraction every time we see each other and that kiss that night on your deck and then in the car today? Whew, I still remember how it made me feel for the rest of the night and I'm still reliving the one from earlier over and over again," she said.

Diesel was ready for this conversation. He wanted her to know what he wanted and only hoped that he didn't press a wrong button with his revelation. He was laying his own cards out on the table.

"I'm interested in you for more than anything casual. I like what I've learned so far and there is no doubt you are gorgeous. There is no need to lie about my physical attraction to you, but I don't want you to think that's all I'm interested in. I didn't move to California in search of any kind of relationship. I'm fresh off of a divorce that I needed to breathe after and that space, I assumed, would be dating without commitment, pretty much friends with benefits, but then there was you. We've sort of fallen into spending time together and nothing about it has been dull. The more I know, the more I want to know. With every kiss we share, I want ten more kisses. I love watching scary movies with you because every time you are frightened, you practically jump into my lap. It's all of you that I want and though I wasn't looking, there was you and you aren't casual to me. I want more and hope you do, too."

Diezel gave up words from his heart. Like her, he'd been hurt before and settled into what life was for him, but now that he'd met her, he was ready to jump back in with both feet. He watched for any doubt or hesitation on Brooklyn's face as she took in what he said and he saw none.

"I know we talked about it before, especially that night of the first kiss on you deck and like you, I wasn't on the market for anything or anyone and then there was you. You have a promise-filled personality that lets me know you're genuine. You care deeply and your heart is on your sleeve. Because of that, I want to tread lightly so that you know for sure that I don't want to be casual with you either. I haven't dated on a serious level since I was married, but again, then there is you and you've changed my mind about distancing myself from matters of the heart. I think my heart is already in it."

"I know what that feels like. We are on the same page," Diezel said.

Sexy thoughts crossed her mind and Brooklyn couldn't help the eager thoughts that crossed her mind thinking about what would be next for them. She used her napkin to wipe her mouth just in case there was any drool on her lips. Diezel was too damn gorgeous for his own good. She eyed him up and down before leaning back in her chair and capturing his eyes.

"Don't get me wrong because every time I see you, I want to literally jump your bones, but I don't want you to think bad of me like I'm some she-devil who thinks that way or wants to do that with every man I meet. There is something about you that is irresistible. What you hear me say on my show is fact. I love men, I love intimacy and with the right man, I want to love,

love. I haven't thought this way in a long time and then there was you."

"You are the sexiest, most desirable woman I've ever met and since we're being all open and honest, you have the most erotic essence about you and all I can think about is having you under me, writhing around, moaning my name, letting me know what makes you feel good," he leaned forward over the table and whispered.

He barely noticed the waitress putting their food on the table. He couldn't shake the fact that she admitted that she wanted to jump him. He knew that now, there was no doubt about what was next for them. They had waited long enough. If he didn't have her soon, he was going to combust on the spot.

"Great, sexy minds think alike then," she said on a whisper, holding his sexually heightened gaze with her own devilish one.

"I'm glad you said it first because I've been working overtime to not remove every stitch of your clothes every time I see you and show you how much I have desired you since the day we met," he admitted. Diezel was finding it hard to swallow as the milky pools of ocean water swaying back and forth, that were her eyes hypnotized him.

Neither of them moved toward eating their food. He could see her breathing had become just as ragged as his at the thought that they'd both been limiting themselves for no reason when making love is clearly what they both wanted.

"Why are we waiting?" Brooklyn asked, not taking her eyes off of his as she unconsciously gripped the edge of the table. She no longer had an appetite for food.

Before the waitress could get far, Diezel got her attention and called her back over. He spoke to her, but kept his eyes on Brooklyn. Her heated gaze was burning a hole right through the very essence of him and he never wanted to look away.

"Can we get this meal to go?" he asked her.

"Excuse me sir?" the waitress asked, not sure she heard him knowing she'd just brought their food.

"Yes. We need this to go, please," Brooklyn chimed in, not looking at the waitress either.

"Five times your tip if you can bag this up in five minutes," he said.

With a quickness, the waitress took their food back and rushed to the back of the restaurant.

"My place?" Brooklyn asked anxiously.

"Definitely. Dee and Dani are in mine. I'll call to let her know that I'll be later than planned," Diezel said as images of him making love to Brooklyn all night surfaced in his mind.

"Much later," Brooklyn added.

Diezel leaned over the table, "much, much later," he said.

As they prepared to stand, the waitress showed up with their food all packaged up and ready for them.

"I added two pieces of our famous carrot cake," the waitress said.

"You've just earned an even bigger tip for reading my mind that we'd need dessert," he said.

Looking at the receipt, Diezel took out several hundred dollars and handed them to the waitress before walking briskly with Brooklyn to the car. They were on a mission.

11

Diezel drove them back to the house in silence, neither needing to say what was next for them. It was clear by how focused they both were on getting back to her house, knowing that the night was going to be explosive. There need for each other could no longer be contained.

Within minutes, he pulled back up to his house not even an hour after leaving and his purpose was clear. There was no more fighting the obvious attraction between him and Brooklyn. He didn't set out to dive right into an intimate relationship with her, but the force pulling them together was stronger than the one keeping them apart. He could hold out forever if he was the only one who felt the steamy connection, but Brooklyn's admission that she was feeling it too and wanted him as much as he wanted her was the only confirmation he needed.

After parking in front of his garage, Diezel pulled out his phone and dialed.

"Dee, is Dani asleep yet?" he asked.

"Yeah, she just fell asleep in my lap while we were watching a movie. I was just about to take her and tuck her in. What's up?"

Diezel turned and saw the ardent look on Brooklyn's face and knew he needed to hurry. He was wasting time when they could be naked.

"Are you good if I'm late? I mean, really, really late like in the morning before it's time to take Dani to camp?" he asked hurriedly.

"Big brother, I saw you pull up to the house on the security camera and I already know what that's code for. You and Brooklyn, huh? We'll be fine. Go have your fun and after a week of being here and getting to know Brooklyn, you've got a winner," she said.

Diezel smiled across the car, but didn't divulge what Dee had said.

"Since you sleep upstairs in the other spare room, take Dani up with you and let her sleep with you. I don't want her to wake up and not see me or you," he said.

"Got you covered and stop worrying. Dani is safe in my care and if for any reason you're not here in the morning, I'll take her to daycare. Where are the spare keeps because you have my car blocked in?" Dee said.

"The spare to my car is on my dresser in the black box, but you won't need them. I don't want to miss dropping her off and getting my morning hug and kiss from her. I'll be right next door if you need me. Make sure the alarm is set and I'll see you in the morning."

Diezel ended the call and turned to Brooklyn.

"Ready?" she asked.

"You have no idea how ready I am. More than you know."

Brooklyn shivered at the sound of his deep, melodious, husky voice. This is what she talked about when she spoke of how she wanted a man to make her feel just by talking to her. All she needed was the sound of the voice of a man who desired her to drive her to bliss. She knew she was more than ready for him and trusted him when he said he was ready for her.

To check for herself, she reached across the car and as her lips met his, her hand slipped to his crotch and found out his assessment of how ready he was couldn't be truer. No woman would be able to resist caressing to feel him swell under her touch and she was no exception.

"I would say you're more than ready, too," she moaned in delight.

Diezel was so turned on by how open Brooklyn was about her need for him that if he didn't soon get out of the car and get into her, he was going to embarrass himself before he was even naked, something he'd never even done as a teenage boy making out in the back of Davis' car with his then girlfriend.

"You're killing me. Let's go, sweetness," he said eagerly, speaking through clinched teeth as he tried to temporarily reign in his need.

Brooklyn would normally wait for him to come around and open her car door, but she was done with formalities because as hot and ready as she knew he was, she was a walking time bomb who was done waiting to get to a powerful explosion. She wanted and needed it sooner rather than later.

Dispensing with the use of her key, Brooklyn used the keypad on the door to enter her code and the minute the door opened and she disabled the alarm, she dropped the purse she was holding and when she saw Diezel's wanting, hooded stare planted squarely on her displaying his animalistic need, she moved when he moved and before she could think, they were kissing as if they were trying to devour each other on the spot. Lips tangled, hands roamed and breathing became secondary as loving became primary.

Brooklyn kicked off her high heels as Diezel pulled his shirt up and out of his pants and then over his head leaving him standing in front of her with a bare chest which was beckoning to her.

"Damn, I could look at you every day like this and it would never get old," she uttered while leaning forward and placing a few soft kisses on his pecs letting him know she wasn't bashful or shy about what she liked and right now she liked the man who stood before her.

"I'm next door any day, any time, baby," Diezel said and picked her up in his arms.

"Bed? he asked.

"To your left," she groaned.

Hating the distance between their lips, Diezel

turned with her in his arms and kissed her with wayward abandonment, sending wave after wave of passion between them as he poured every bit of lust he had for her into it. The kiss only ended when they reached the bedroom and he sat her back down on her feet. He reached down and gathered her face into both of his hands, planting one soft, sweet kiss after another on her lips and enjoying the mewling sounds that escaped after each one.

"I would believe that you were a dream if I wasn't actually touching and kissing you like this," Diezel said as he slid the thin straps of Brooklyn's dress from her shoulders and down her arms, letting his eyes follow the path it took to the floor. "You're real and I'm the luckiest guy in the world right now," he said.

He looked from her feet, to her long legs, up to her breasts which were enclosed by a sexy, silky black strapless bra, then up to her mouth that called to him wanting more.

"I'm just as real as you are," Brooklyn said, adoringly.

As she reached for his belt and the snap of his pants, her heart sped up the moment Diezel released the back clasp on her bra and her globes landed in his waiting hands. She loved the rough, yet smooth feel of the pads of his fingers as he caressed and molded them to his touch. She thought she would lose her mind watching his head dip as he paid extra attention to first one hard pebbled nipple and then the other. As he massaged one with his mouth, he rolled the other between his finger, giving it a little pinch and feeling the zing flow from her, back to him as she squirmed under his touch.

Diezel felt his pants fall to the floor and his hips moved of their own volition when Brooklyn reached inside of his boxers and stroked his growing manhood. Her hands felt as velvety as her lips now felt against his mouth when he leaned up for a searing kiss, finally moving them to topple onto the bed. Having her under him had been in his dreams, but now he was with her, live and in living color and no dream could ever measure up to being with her in reality.

Before covering her body with his, he wanted to remove the last bit of clothing that kept him from seeing all of her. Kissing his way down her chest from her breasts to her flat, toned stomach, he kissed around the thin straps of her lacy black panties and followed her hips as they moved slowly from side to side. He heard her breath hiss when he used his teeth to pull the thin material down her legs, stopping briefly to plant a kiss on the very thin strip of hair she left remaining after her waxing earlier in the day. She whispered a silent thanks to herself for her trip to the spa.

Once Diezel had Brooklyn's panties off, he used his hands to caress her, starting at her feet and working his way up her legs. He then used his hands to roam all over her body as if he were examining her for any imperfections, knowing he wouldn't find any. Her beautiful skin was soft and pliant under his caress and he couldn't wait to feel it as their bodies rubbed together.

Before joining her back on the bed, he reached for his pants and removed the two condoms he'd placed there. He didn't usually walk around with condoms, but he didn't trust he'd be able to be out with Brooklyn and not want to be inside of her. He was glad he decided to play it safe.

"I'm glad you have condoms on you because even though I haven't used any in a long time, I picked up some the other day and they wouldn't fit you," she said acknowledging his length and girth. "I'll assume those are magnums," she added and smiled when he held up the gold packs for her to see.

"Too bad I didn't bring more because I think two just won't due with you. On the other hand, there's so much more I'd love to do to you that won't require one," he said.

To prove his point, before sliding up her body, Diezel spread her legs, bearing all of her glorious womanhood to his view. Without preparing her for what he had planned, he leaned forward and while keeping his eyes on hers as she tried to focus on what he was doing, he snaked his tongue out and swiped up her glistening womanhood which was already drenched and waiting for him.

Brooklyn couldn't see and since she couldn't, she closed her eyes and felt.

"Yes!" she screamed and then covered her mouth as if she were trying to silence herself.

"Don't hold back with me, ever. I want to hear you scream," Diezel said and then licked her again. This time, he spread her womanly lips open and used his fingers to spread her essence around as he used his tongue to stroke the hard nub that came out to greet him. Focusing on it, he went between licking and sucking making sure his head didn't lose connection with her as her hips began moving around wildly under him. His own body was on fire as the liquid essence from her body coated his lips, reminding him of how turned on she was, absolutely matching his current state of hardened arousal. He wanted to be inside of her so bad, but he noticed how fast her hips were now moving and the way she went between screaming and moaning, he wouldn't dare stop giving her the pleasure they both wanted. Seeing her in the throes of passion gave to him as much as he was giving to her.

Brooklyn was out of her mind. She'd never had a man pay as much attention and find the exact spots to caress with his hands, mouth and tongue. She had no idea she could feel this good. Her mind was crazy and her body began to build with the feeling that she was about to explode. She wanted to hold on to the feeling as long as possible as his tongue continued licking and kissing her intimately, driving her mad with want and before she had a chance to think about what was happening, her body did explode as she moved about wildly on the bed while white streaks of light shot across her closed eyes. She tried to grip the blanket, but instead one hand reached for Diezel's head and she held on to his bald head as her hips moved uncontrollably. She did what Diezel said and she screamed like a banshee in the forest not caring who could hear her.

Diezel didn't let up even after Brooklyn's orgasm slammed through her. He gave her more and more for as long as her hips moved against his face. When her body finally calmed back onto the bed, he kissed his way up her legs and then to her mouth, allowing her to have a taste of herself from his lips.

"You taste amazing," he whispered in her ear as he kissed his way around her face and neck as he watched her struggle to catch her breath.

Allowing her a few seconds to gather herself, he reached for one of the condoms and placed the other on the table next to the bed. Ripping the pack open, he quickly covered his straining flesh before covering her body with his. He smiled when she opened her eyes and looked up into his face.

"I feel like I should say thank you because I've never, ever exploded like that before. I mean never," Brooklyn admitted.

"Never?" he asked curiously.

"You are what I talk about wanting and not what I've ever gotten. That was amazing," she declared.

Spreading her legs to move his body between them, Diezel first kissed her lips and then positioned himself at her entrance with his body aflame with a need so great, his vision was already blurry, something that typically happened after an orgasm, not before one. Brooklyn was setting off all kinds of sirens in his body.

"I am here to please baby and we're just beginning. If there is anything your body desires, all you have to do is tell me. This playground tonight is open for satisfying every need you have," he expressed deeply.

"What about your needs?" she asked, sheepishly.

"I'm about to satisfy that right now," he said and with ease, he slid inside of her body, immediately realizing the tightness and took his time. He gave her one glorious inch at a time of his nine, knowing that if she hadn't indulged in a while, she needed time to get accustomed to his size.

The first feel of her almost had him losing control the minute he entered her. They moaned and groaned together as he looked down between them at the sight of his body entering hers slowly, one inch at a time. Kissing her deeply as a flood of emotion poured through him, Diezel surged forward, finally giving her all of him as he felt Brooklyn grip his shoulders as her nails dug into his skin, driving him even wilder. His hips moved in sync with hers as they trembled through the pleasure together. He held her gaze as he used his eyes to send signals promising her that what they were sharing was never to be a one-time thing. Now that he's had her, he had no plans of going back to not having her. Wrapping her legs around his hips, he increased the pace as the bed rocked and creaked under the pressure of their unrestrained movements.

"I'm there, Diezel!" Brooklyn screamed as she pushed her hips up to meet his thrusts, giving him every bit of the same level of gratification that he was giving to her.

"I'm right with you, baby. Mmm, I can't get enough of you," Diezel whispered as he himself got closer and closer to letting go. He spoke soft, but forceful words in her ear to express what her body was doing to his and what it felt like to have her body gripping his tightly as he surged in and out of her body.

Brooklyn's body couldn't hold off any more as Diezel screamed her name. Her mind and body exploded with an earth-shattering orgasm, causing her hips to writhe wildly on the bed, holding on to him to be sure he was real. He felt real between her legs and in her arms.

Diezel let go and allowed his orgasm to quake again and again, soaring to heights he'd never experienced before and he relished in gigantic proportions of pleasure he never knew existed. He rode the wave of pure ecstasy as his jaw twitched and his climax went on and on. He lived in it, delighted in it and in the lust-filled words Brooklyn expressed to him as their bodies calmed.

They stayed that way, intimately connected as they each tried to get control of their ragged breaths.

"Pinch me so that I know that I'm still alive," Diezel finally said.

"I can't because I don't know if I have any feeling in any part of my body. Every sensor in my body is on overload at the moment and I love it. I can't tell you how amazing that was."

"Ditto, baby," Diezel said still working on his breathing. Could it be that this is the kind of love making he thought he had been experiencing, but only really experienced with Brooklyn tonight? He had definitely been missing out. Every fiber of his being was alert and now aware. He leaned up and looked Brooklyn in the eyes. "You were well worth the wait and not just the wait for the past few weeks since we've met. I'm talking about well worth the wait of thirty-one years. This is what making love to the perfect woman is like," he said, kissing her sweetly while smiling inwardly.

"And then there was you," Brooklyn said against his lips.

"And then there was you," Diezel replied.

12

"The brothers are in the house!" Dalton shouted as he and Detrick entered Davis' house finding Davis and Diezel sitting out on the back deck enjoying their beers.

"It's about time!" Diezel said standing and going into the house to greet his brothers. For the first time in a long time, the four of them were in the same place. As greetings and hugs went all around, they admired how good they each looked.

"I can't believe we're actually all together," Davis said.

"Hey, I'm always trying to connect with each of you, but everyone's always so busy. I'm glad we could carve out time to hang out for a few days," Dietrick said.

"What are we getting into for the next few days?" Dalton asked, going out on the deck and grabbing a beer from the cooler.

As the brothers all gathered on the deck, Dietrick reached down and picked up Denim who ran through the house and joined them.

"Hold on to him because he's my little escape artist. If you turn your head for a second he'll try and slip out either to the beach or next door," Diezel said. After he spoke, all eyes turned to him and there was silence.

"Next door, huh? Davis told us about you and his neighbor, the famous Brooklyn Hunter also known as the 'Brooklyn Bombshell'. She is fine, bro. How did you hook up with her?" Dalton asked.

"I didn't hook up with her. I'm in a relationship with her which is beyond hooking up."

"Sounds serious," Dietrick said.

"I think it is," Davis said. "I arrived yesterday and he and I had a chance to talk after Dee and Dani went to bed and I have never, ever heard him talk about a woman the way he talks about her. I'm thinking there is something serious going on here," he added.

"Damn right it is and I'm knocking out anyone who tries to make light of it. I know I haven't had the best of luck with women and my last committed relationship was my marriage, but Brooklyn is different. I would never talk down about Jessica because she's Dani's mother, but Brooklyn is the kind of woman I've been wanting and I mean the whole package, brains and beauty, a heart of gold and a love for life like no woman I've ever met," Diezel explained.

"Brooklyn Hunter from the radio with that hot, hot late-night talk show?" Dalton asked.

"The very one and she's mine," Diezel said, gloating. He knew that men all around the country wanted the sultry beauty, but he had her and he couldn't be happier.

After their night and early morning together a few

weeks back, they had been pretty much inseparable since then. They had finally gotten around to a full date night out that included dinner and a movie and they weren't distracted by thoughts of ripping each other's clothes off. There first attempt at a real date turned into getting their food to go and then devouring each other for an entire night where neither of them got a wink of sleep.

Since Delia decided to spend the entire summer with him, they'd gone out often while she watched Dani. He also loved how well Brooklyn and Dani go along. Some of their best nights were grilling out on the deck with the four of them laughing and telling jokes. They allowed Dani to talk them into playing card games with no rules or with her made up rules and still it was a lot of fun.

"What does all this mean? You're in love with her?" Dietrick asked.

"Yes, I am and I knew if from the start, but after these past two months, I have no doubt she is exactly what I want."

"How does it feel to have her talk so intimately on the radio at night? Do you wonder if she's talking about the relationship the two of you have?" Dalton asked.

"I feel fine about it and if she did talk about our relationship, there wouldn't be any love problems again with any of her callers. When I tell you she is the perfect woman for me, it's not a joke. Her parents are coming in next week for a few days to visit and she wants me to meet them. I've talked to her mother on the phone and she seems delighted that Brooklyn is happy and she thanked me for making her daughter smile again. I'm telling you guys, she's the one," Diezel said.

"The one, again?" Dietrick exclaimed.

"Yeah, we've heard that before," Dalton laughed.

Davis was the only one who didn't find the comment humorous.

"You know, none of us have heard that before. After mom and pop died, we all had our struggles in how we dealt with it. Dalton, you decided on a whim to move to Colorado where we didn't know anyone and I didn't even know people lived their other than to visit in order to ski. You worked in a bar, for god sake and refused to come visit any of us for almost a year. Dietrick, if it hadn't been for a few connections pop had with the NYPD, you'd be in jail after reckless driving and street racing cars. Yes, Diezel met a girl and ran off to Vegas and married her after a month or two of sex, something that I could say was a regret, but we have Dani and we love Dani with everything in us, so no regrets there. Me, I took on the role as the caretaker for the entire clan at my age and that was a lot including dealing with our fifteen-year-old sister. We didn't have a lot of family, but even they couldn't handle her and after being passed around from one aunt to the next, she became our sole responsibility. I locked myself away and focused on work, making that my whole world and yet here we all are, alive and doing well. Diezel has always been the one to fall for girls quickly and wears his heart on his sleeve like mom always did. If he says she's the one, I believe him and I support him. Besides that, I've lived next door to Brooklyn for three years and she's an incredible person. She and Diezel make a perfect couple and when I say I have experienced their love after only a day, I mean it. You should see them together," Davis said.

"I'm happy for you, Diez," Dietrick said. "If anyone is going to be in love, it should be you. I'm never falling in love. I want to make sure every woman who wants to experience some of me gets an equal share. I don't want anything like love being the reason I have to deny any of them," he laughed.

"The epitome of a playboy," Dalton said shaking his head.

"You should talk. I don't remember hearing about you being seriously involved with anyone. Your life is that fire department," Davis said.

"Yeah, big brother, well what about you? You've been involved with Delaney for a few years now and not once have I ever heard you say you're in love with her. Why she sticks around, I don't know," Dalton said.

"What I have with Lanie is complicated, but it works," Davis explained.

"What you meant to say is it works for you. Delaney is ready to get married and drop baby after baby, but we all know the hang-up is you," Dietrick exclaimed.

Davis chose not to respond. He and Delaney were having problems, very big problems and though he knew he was the cause, he didn't want to bring up the subject with his brothers. Instead, he wanted to focus on the few days they had together and he hoped by the time he returned to Milan to join her, that she'd still be there. Right now, he wasn't so sure she would be. Why did women have to hear the word love to know that they were loved?

"Whatever. We've all dealt with struggles in the love department, hence a room full of successful, single men," Davis confirmed.

"Are you saying we messed up our own lives by not getting counseling after mom and pop died?" Dalton asked.

"I'm saying the only person who did get counseling is Dee because we all made her, but we all probably could have used it. I don't want to spend the next few days talking about where we fall short. This is the first time in a long time we've been together and I want it to be about fun. Agreed?" Davis asked looking at each of his brothers.

"Agreed," they said collectively.

"Good," Dalton said, "now, where is my niece? I can't believe she's far from Denim?" he added.

"She and Dee are next door with Brooklyn. They're

planning some kind of girl's night in with nail painting, facials and ice cream. They're spending the night next door," Diezel said.

"So, Dani likes Brooklyn?" Dietrick asked.

"Yes, she does. She likes her a lot and I love seeing them together. Our last night together, I'm going to have some friends from the office over, Davis is inviting some friends and Brooklyn has a few friends she's going to invite over for a big barbecue. We have never had all of us including Dee and Dani all together in the same house since right after Dani was born. That alone is a reason to celebrate," Diezel said.

"We also want to celebrate you and Brooklyn. She's brought life back to your face and into your life and that is a major reason to celebrate. Jessica took you through a lot and for you to really be in love, I want to embrace it. I want us all to embrace it because we may have extended family, but as far as immediate family, we are all we have," Davis said.

"What's on tap for tonight?" Dietrick asked.

"Dinner, drinks and gambling at Hollywood Park Casino. There are table games and some of the best food you've ever had. Drinks will be flowing all night and I'm looking forward to hanging with my brothers. We're going to have the perfect brothers' night out. The girls are covered and I've got my brothers in town. I'm talking this is a perfect night and I'm ready!" Diezel shouted.

"Nice. Let's call an Uber because none of us will be

able to drive back and let's get this night started. I'm glad we're all here. Let's make the best of it. We've come a long way from where our lives were over five years ago. It's good to see you," Davis said.

Diezel nodded in accord. The moment he knew everyone was coming in, his excitement escalated. His life was on track with Brooklyn and he couldn't be happier and now he had his brothers together. He couldn't wait for them to all be together, knowing that Brooklyn will fit in nicely with the brood. He also looked forward to meeting her parents.

He remembered talking to her parents, especially her mother and he had no hesitation when he let her know that he was in love with Brooklyn, something he wouldn't hesitate to tell Brooklyn when the time was right.

They were enjoying the life together as a couple and when he wasn't working and she was caught up on sleep, they found fun and exciting activities to do.

Recently, Dee had gone into Hollywood to sightsee and go on one of those TMZ Hollywood tour buses. He, Dani and Brooklyn donned their bathing suits and after putting Denim in his plush towel covered carrier, they spent the day on the beach. Several times when he got up to take Dani to the water, Brooklyn asked him to let her do it. After an hour, Dani had fallen asleep and after laying her out under the umbrella on the blanket, shading her from the sun, they sat and talked about how their relationship was going. When she expressed how happy she had been since they'd started dating, he told her she was more than he could have asked for. He hadn't smiled this much in a long time and it was because of his two favorite girls, her and Dani.

Besides dating and spending time on the beach and other outings, he enjoyed their down time at night with Dani and then once he'd put her to bed, they didn't always make love, but instead loved cuddling out on the deck enjoying the still of the night. They didn't have many nights to spend in each other's arms because of Brooklyn's late-night schedule, but when they could, they loved relaxing after his long days of work and her long nights and love making became second nature. He didn't have to guess when she needed him and he never let doubt creep in about his need and desire for her. They had all begun to settle into life as a family.

Dee was a major help since she arrived and now that he agreed that she could move to Los Angeles and stay with him after she graduated in a year, she was already calling California her home and had already begun making friends after signing up for group acting classes.

Dani was happy, he was happy, Brooklyn was happy and life couldn't be better. The only issue he had was that after two months, he had only heard from Jessica once and she talked to Dani for a minute.

"Let's get moving guys," Davis said, interrupting his

AND THEN THERE WAS YOU

thoughts.

Diezel pushed thoughts of Jessica from his mind and focused on his brothers.

"I need to shower and change," Dalton said.

"We all do. This is a night we're hanging out in our best so, y'all know what to do," Davis said.

"Diezel was more than ready. Life was good and he was feeling good about it.

13

"Dani, I don't have time for this right now. Go get your father and tell him I want to talk to him right now."

"But, mommy. I want to show you my new doll Ms. Brooklyn got me. Don't you want to see it?" Dani said sadly, now holding her head down and no longer looking at the anger on her mother's face on the cellphone screen.

"I don't want to see any doll some strange woman got you. What did I tell you about talking to strangers? You know better than that. Where's your father? I'm sick of him," Jessica hollered.

"But..but..she's nice, mommy and daddy likes her."

"Oh, does he? That doesn't mean you have to. Go get him."

"He's making me a sandwich."

"Go get him now!" Jessica screamed into the phone causing Dani to drop it and run out of her bedroom and right to Diezel where she grabbed his legs tight and held on as she began to cry.

Diezel wiped his hands and reached down to pick her up. He tried to hold her out so that he could look in her face to talk about why she was cry, but all she wanted was for him to hold her tight, so that's what he did.

"Whoa. What's wrong, Sweetpea? Tell daddy why you're crying," he said, already having an idea. After not hearing from her mother, she'd finally called to facetime with Dani and it looks like the conversation didn't go well. Why are you crying?" he asked concerned.

"Mommy screamed really loud. She's mad at me for my doll."

"What?" he asked confused.

Dani didn't explain further. Instead, she grabbed him tight around the neck and held on as if she needed protection. Walking toward the bedroom, he saw his cellphone on the floor and could hear Jessica screaming at the top of her lungs. Before he could make out much of what she was saying, he heard one curse word after the other and knew Dani didn't need to be present.

"Daddy," Dani mumbled in his ear as she laid her head on his shoulder. Stepping back out of the room, he called for his sister who was upstairs getting dressed to go shopping.

"Dee, come get Dani for a few minutes," he yelled up the stairs. Within seconds, she appeared and took Dani from his arms.

"What's wrong with her?" she asked seeing a look of terror on Dani's face.

"Jessica is what happened, but it's going to be okay, right?" he said in his happy voice. He didn't want to terrorize Dani any more than Jessica already had.

Dee shook her head and turned to head back up the steps.

"You're fine. You want to help aunt Dee pick out something to wear?" Delia say cheerfully.

Dani shook her head yes and grabbed her doll tighter.

Delia looked at Diezel, reassuring him that she knew what was going on and that she'd look after Dani while he handled business.

Going back into Dani's bedroom, he could still hear Jessica screaming and cursing on the other end of the phone as he picked it up.

"What is wrong with you? What did you say to Dani? She came running into the kitchen crying saying you were mad at her about a doll? Are you out of your mind? She's four? What about a doll could you be mad about?" he tried to ask calmly, yet spoke through clenched teeth.

"Who the hell is this woman you have around my daughter and letting her buy her gifts? My daughter doesn't need anything from any of those tramps you're out there doing in California!"

"First of all, fix your tone and your attitude and second, our daughter didn't deserve to be on the other end of your wrath."

"I told her to get you and she still wanted to talk. She wasn't listening to me just like you don't!"

"I'm not one of your children, so my listening to you or not is not on my list of priorities. Our daughter is four years old and if you have something you need to talk to me about, feel free to direct your anger towards me, but don't you ever raise your voice to her to the point where she terrified. As for the woman, her name is Brooklyn and if you would answer the phone when I call or return any of my calls or texts, you would have known about her by now. I guess I'm asking too much of Dani's mother to stay in contact and at least say hello to her daughter," he said pointedly.

"If you wanted me to know about some woman, you would have said so in your many messages."

"My messages were always about you taking a few minutes to talk to your daughter in between your trips to Atlantic City and your nights in the club. If you don't want me to call you so that Dani can talk to you, I will avoid dialing your number, but you can feel free to call her whenever you want to talk to her, but you are never to terrorize our daughter or yell at her like some maniac."

"I don't want any of your women around my daughter," Jessica said.

"What I do with my daughter when she's with me and who I have around her is none of your business. Again, I tried to connect with you several times over the past two months that Dani has been here and this is the first time you actually answered your phone. I wanted Dani to have time to talk to you and catch you up on the past two months, but I'm seeing that wasn't a good idea. You instead want to focus on me and my life."

"I don't care anything about you or your life. I care about who you have around my daughter."

"Oh, you didn't care what was going on for the past two months after I've called you two dozen times? You can't play babysitter from New York when you barely do it when Dani is in New York. Now, not that I owe you an explanation, I will tell you that Brooklyn is my girlfriend, someone I've fallen in love with and Dani adores her and she adores Dani. You can't dictate my personal life and Dani and Brooklyn getting to know each other is important to me."

"I don't give two shakes about what's important to you or that you're in love. What are you going to do? Run off and marry her like you did me and then then leave?" Jessica said in a voice letting him know she was irritated with their conversation.

"Again, my personal life is none of your business and I don't complain about men you bring around Dani, though with your mother having her weeks at a time, I guess her being with your mother is better than you parading man after man around Dani."

"Oh, like you don't parade women around Dani?" she asked.

"Brooklyn is the first woman I have ever allowed around Dani, so don't go there. Besides that, Brooklyn is a wonderful woman and I would never have anyone around her that I wouldn't trust. Not that I haven't dated other trustworthy women, but Brooklyn is different and so yes, Dani will be around her. Your only concern should be for Dani, but that's not what this is, is it?" Diezel asked.

He already knew Jessica's anger was at him moving on and not about Dani being around anyone.

"I didn't mean to holler at Dani. I was angry. She's gone all summer and I miss her and then I hear some other woman is buying her dolls that she loves," Jessica said calmer.

"You didn't send any of the things she loves playing with at home. Your mother said she waited as long as she could for you to bring Dani's things only to find that you were in Atlantic City. If you have something you want Dani to have from home, let me know and I will pay for the shipping. This isn't a competition and everyone knows you're Dani's mother, especially Dani, but don't take your anger out on her, ever. I will tell you anything you need to know about Brooklyn, not just because you want to know. She'd thirty and she works as a radio talk-show host."

"Wait, Brooklyn? Are you talking about Brooklyn Hunter from that popular late-night radio show? The woman who looks like Kim Kardashian?" Jessica asked.

"Yes, that's her."

"Were you seeing her when we were together? Is she why you moved to California?"

"No, Jess. I met her when I moved here. She lives next door to my brother. I never stepped out on you when we were married, though we were both unhappy. That's not who I am and you know that. I tried and you know that too, even if you won't admit it. We tried co-parenting when I lived in New York and you wouldn't let me be happy. You showed up on my job, when I was out on a date and pretty much everywhere I went. I understand there is hurt and I felt that distance is what was needed for you to be able to move on. I hate the thought of being away from Dani when I have to take her back to New York, but her seeing us always arguing and fighting wasn't good for either of us. I love Dani more than anything or anyone in this world. I wouldn't do anything that wasn't best for her."

"Well, in the future, if you're going to have a woman around her, I'd like to know. I like Brooklyn's radio show and she seems like a nice person."

"She is," he replied.

"I didn't mean to holler at Dani. I feel like I'm angry all the time."

"You seem angry all the time and I'm sorry for that. I've tried to keep things cordial. I give you whatever you ask for when it comes to Dani. The courts told me I didn't have to pay child support for the three months that Dani is with me each summer, yet I made the decision to do so. You get more than any judge says you should have because you're raising my daughter. I don't interfere in your life nor do I tell you how to live your life. I do ask that we both put Dani first. Her well-being is the most important thing between us. I can't and won't apologize for moving on. Dani is a happy little girl and she needs two parents who love on her all the time. Yes, she's away from you for the summer, but you can facetime her every day all day if you want to. You can call her, all day, every day and I'll make sure she's on the other end. Don't ignore her like you've been doing just to spite me. She doesn't deserve that."

Diezel was angry and finally got the chance to say everything that had been pent up for weeks. He could here Jessica sighing on the other end of the phone and he hoped he was getting through to her. They have struggled with being oil and water for years and now was the perfect time to say enough was enough.

"Where is she? Can I talk to her and apologize?" Jessica asked.

"She's upstairs with Delia. I'll take the phone up for you to talk to her. I know you may have issues with Brooklyn, but Dani likes her. She's good to our daughter and so when she wants to tell you about the fun things she's doing, some will include Brooklyn, so her name may come up. Feel free to be angry at me or judge me, but make your conversations with Dani ones that she will remember and not have nightmares over. When she came running to me, I saw a look of pure terror and shame on her face like she'd done something wrong. Now, I've let you take your anger out on me and I accept that and will take it in place of Dani on any given day, but make that the last time you shout at our daughter for no reason or make her sad about wanting to share something with you that makes her happy and I don't care who gave her a present. Your conversations with her should leave her feeling like she's the princess that she is. Make every conversation about her," he explained and hope he was getting through to her.

Diezel didn't usually release his anger on Jessica, but when it comes to his daughter, he would slay anyone when it came to her and that includes Jessica. He was expecting a barrage of curse words and images of her whipping her neck and pointing her finger as she screamed at the top of her lungs at him for telling her what she can and cannot do when it comes to their daughter, but he didn't hear anything. The phone went silent and he saw her move her face away from the screen. For a second, he thought she'd hung up on him. Still, he waited. The next move was hers and either she would see where she was wrong or he would spend an eternity straightening her out if need be. Dani was his world and he expected more from her mother.

"I hear you and I'm sorry for screaming at her and making her think it was wrong to love her new doll. I'm sorry, Diez. Can I talk to her, please?" Jessica asked.

Diezel took the steps two at a time and found Dani and Delia staring at a mound of clothes.

"She's helping me pick out something to wear," Delia said.

"Looks like it's not working," he laughed.

"Auntie Dee has a lot of clothes, daddy."

"I know and she's only been here a few weeks. Mommy is on the phone for you," he said and Dani's smile went away. He reached the phone to her. "She's sorry," he mouthed.

"Mommy is sorry, Dani," Jessica said loud enough for Dani to hear.

Dani took the phone. "Hi, mommy."

"Hi. Look, mommy is sorry for how I talked to you. I didn't mean it. I was having a bad day and I should always be nice to you. You are my pumpkin. You want to finish telling me all about the fun you're having with daddy? I want to see your doll so you have to hold her up so I can see, okay?"

Diezel smiled and nodded when Dani looked at him and then she started talking to get in two months of fun. He turned and went back down the steps to finish making lunch. He would leave Dani in the room with his sister in case Jessica slipped up again. He had no doubt his baby sister would give Jessica a tongue lashing that would make what he said to her look like kid's plat. There was something to be learned from the phone encounter with Jessica. He didn't know how he was going to survive when Dani was back in New York. He dreaded having to take her back.

Going back downstairs, he hated that their happiness was interrupted by more of Jessica's drama. They'd just spent the weekend before with all of his brothers in town and on their last night, they had a house full of people and partied until the wee hours of the morning. Davis had invited friends and so did Brooklyn. He smiled thinking that Robin finally got her wish and got to meet his other two brothers, the beefy crew, she called them. By the end of the night, with no effort at all, Brooklyn had one over the last two members of her family. That night had gone well and so did a few days later when Brooklyn's parents had come to town.

Brooklyn had been nervous because he was the first guy she'd ever really introduced to them. When she'd met Max, it had been at some celebrity party and they dated in secret until right before she told her parents she and Max were getting married. She was happy to be adult about her relationship with Diezel.

Her parents reminded him so much of his own parents that it was scary. What he loved the most was how they loved Dani. Not having any grandchildren, they loved spending two days of Dani winning them over.

At the end of their last night in town, he and Brooklyn's dad sat out on his deck late that evening and talked about Brooklyn and he accepted the thank you from her father for being the kind of man she needed in her life. He let her father know that Brooklyn brought out the best in him. He liked that they couldn't be happier that he and Brooklyn had found each other. No one was happier than he was. To now have Jessica complain about Brooklyn buying Dani a doll that she loved, he was angry that he let her take him to a place he hated going. No more would he deal with Jessica and her mess. They needed to have a heart to heart about how to co-parent Dani. Though he thought he had a plan in place, he was no second-guessing that.

14

"I'm back y'all and we're ready for our last topic for discussion tonight before we go into two hours of some of the best love making music ever created. Before we do that, our last topic is about music. I want to hear from you about the song or songs that get your blood flowing when you're with your significant other. I know we all have a list of songs we'd like to have on rotation when we think about kissing, caressing and having our clothes slowly removed or ripped off in a sexual haze so intoxicating that you can't wait to get naked. I'm like that especially now that I think about that incredibly sexy hunk of a man I've been seeing. I won't tell y'all his business, but let me tell you he is about business and we don't need any music. All I need are the sweet sounds of our love making and I'm in my zone. I do have certain songs I love listening to when I'm in a sexy mood. Now, don't clown a sister on this first one and I'm going to share three or four with you really quick. The first is *"Sexy Can I"* by Ray J. Some of you are saying how can she consider that a mood song with its upbeat tempo, but the truth is, that is one of the sexiest sounding songs and beats I know. That man is asking permission for all the ways he wants to take a woman – he's putting it out there and not just doing it. Isn't it sexy when a man verbally tells you what he wants to do to you, how he wants to do it and how he knows it's going to make you feel? When I hear that song, I want to go out and get a stripper pole and plant it right in the center of my bedroom. When my man enters, I want to be in something slinky and sexy and pretty much barely-there. I want to invite him to sit down while I show him all the tricks and flips I know how to do, setting the tone for the evening and the perfect song is, *"Sexy Can I"*. At that moment, my response will be a loud, booming yes as I show him what the image of him having his way with me makes me feel. Have you listened to that song before? If not, I'm going to make sure I play it tonight and when I do, I want you to close your eyes and see in your mind what he's saying and then tell me you don't want to hop up and go in search of your mate for some hot like fire mating! Caller, you're on the air? What's your song before I give y'all my next pick."

Brooklyn exhaled and picked up the papers in front of her and began fanning. With the microphone on mute, she smiled at Robin who was also fanning across the table from her.

"Girl, that man has you sprung!" she said.

"I can't begin to tell you what Diezel does for me. It's indescribable!" she said going back to listening to her caller.

"Brooklyn, this is Imani and I have a song that was made before I was born and the artist had also died before I was born. The song is *"Til Tomorrow"* by Marvin Gaye. One night, my then boyfriend who is now my husband and I were on the verge of breaking up. It was a few years ago when I was twenty-six and we were having childish issues, but this night we had gone out and had a big fight. I was through with all the drama and wanted out. He drove me home that night and I told him to come inside and get his things that he'd left and that since he didn't want to do right, we were finished. Once inside, I went to the bedroom to gather some clothes and other things he'd left and when I came back out into the living room, he had turned on the radio and that song started playing. I was about to speak when the music started playing and then I started listening to the words. He started listening too and while the song played, we stood staring at each other. By the end of the song, we were naked right in the living room and going at it against the wall. We've been together ever since. That song helped us realize how much we really loved each other and we didn't want drama coming between the love we knew we had for each other. We still play that song, not to get in the mood, but to remember how that song led to our forever love," Imani said.

"Imani, girl, now that's what I'm talking about. I love that song and I love having it on heavy rotation. Did y'all hear Imani's hot story? If I wasn't working right now, I'd be home wrapped around my man with that song playing over the speakers. I love it! Who's next?" she asked and hit the button for the next caller.

"Brooklyn baby, this is Tyler and for me, it's *"Candy Shop"* by 50 Cent". A lot of people will say it's because of how sexual the lyrics are and that's part of it, but the biggest draw for me is not only is it a man saying what he likes, but the woman is saying what she wants and what she likes. Watching my girl wind her hips to that beat and telling what will happen when she takes me to the candy shop. I'm just saying, as soon as I hang up the phone, I'm going to find that song and me and my girl are about to make our neighbors very unhappy. I hope they have their noise-cancelling headphones on," Tyler laughed.

"Now, Tyler, you are setting my phone line on fire tonight with that story. The *"Candy Shop"* is a hot song and I've never looked at a lollipop the same way after hearing it. I am also a fan. I'm telling you, I'm writing down all of these songs and I'm making sure I add them to my playlist. I love, love and I love everything about it, especially when it comes to how to keep the fire in a relationship burning hot all the time. Music is important in life and it's important in love, too. Sometimes words from a song allow people to relay feelings without saying a word. Perhaps they aren't good with expressing themselves, but a song does it effortlessly for them. I'm all for whatever works in your life. Let me share my number two song. That would be *"Rock Wit'cha"* by Bobby Brown. That song is soft, smooth, hot and he rocks it like no one else could and once I saw that video, I was all in. When I think of that song, I think of a romantic night with candles lit. Did y'all catch that scene in the video when he calls her thickness? Ooh, that makes my skin tingle. I'm going to do a show about pet names and find out what are those names you like to call your significant other. Wouldn't you like to be on the other end of a man who can't wait for you to get to him so that he can love all on you? I know I would love to be that woman who desired my man so much that if I missed being with him when I planned and when I finally got to him, he was hot and ready for me. Y'all are starting something up in this studio tonight. I'm going to hit you with my third simply because I'm on a roll right now. Check out this hot, steamy number. I'm talking about Johnny Gill's hit, *"Behind Closed Doors."* Now that's a song for lovers."

Brooklyn squirmed in her chair as Robin laughed at her. She could barely get her next words out when Robin held up a piece of paper with a note on it just for her. It read, "Don't mess up that chair squirming around. No orgasms in the station chairs." Brooklyn practically choked. She was definitely close because all she could think about was Diezel and picturing all hot, hard and ready for her. She waved Robin off and went back to her show.

"Hey guys, all I have to say is, we all do it and we all love it. We may not want everyone to know what goes on behind our closed doors with our love, but when it's really hot and your desire is on a level so high you're not sure you ever want to come down, there is nothing that two lovers can't imagine doing to set that moment off right. Some things you may share with your girls or with your homeboys, but I know there are some elicit, downright erotic and amatory, intimate encounters that you don't tell anyone about because they are too hot to share. I've met a man, ladies, who rings my bell every time. He leaves me stuttering and then passed out in a coma and the more I melt under his touch, the more touches I want to experience. *"Behind Closed Doors"* has me thinking about all kinds of acrobatics he and I could do and all the ways our bodies could twist and turn as we sweat it out all night long. I can't say that I've ever felt this voracious, insatiable or ravenous in my life and now when women talk about having their worlds rocked, I can relate! What about you? Let's take a quick break and I'm coming back with a tall glass of ice water and we'll be ready to hear from our next caller. I see these lines are all lit up. You've got three minutes to cool off before we heat things back up again," Brooklyn said and then muted her microphone as her producer put on a song.

"Brooklyn, you are killing it tonight," Terry said.

Brooklyn gave her producer the thumbs up and turned to Robin.

"What?" she said when Robin sat before her with her mouth wide open.

"What do you mean what? That was hot! I mean it was off the charts. What is Diezel doing to you, girl?" she asked and laughed.

"Everything and then some," she said and laughed. She was about to get up to stretch her legs and calm her body that drummed and ached for Diezel like never before. They had been spending more and more time together and times when they got their alone time, she never wanted to go back to the world. No man had ever done the things to her body like he did and the more she got, the more she needed and wanted, like now. All this sex talk and she was ready to take an extended break and race home to see Diezel for a quick minute or more like a quick hour.

She was about to stand when her cellphone pinged with a text message. She wondered who it could be sending her a text after midnight. She smiled and her sex jumped when she saw Diezel's name appear on the screen. Her fingers automatically began to shake in anticipation of the things that were running through her mind that she wanted to say. She only had two minutes left, but she could get it in. She put in her code and read the message.

"Hey, beautiful. Guess what I'm listening to?"

"What?" she replied and bit her lower lip in anticipation.

Before ever meeting Diezel, she'd never sex-texted before and yet she was now a big fan because he was so good at it.

"Your show."

"Don't you have a big day in court tomorrow?" she asked.

"I'm having a bigger night right now and it's because of you. How am I supposed to sleep after hearing your show tonight and picturing you swinging on a pole in the middle of your bedroom and then riding mine?"

Brooklyn dropped her phone. It felt hot in her hands after his last text caused her mind to go to him sitting in his room naked and stroking. She loved that he loved doing that and the image had her body running rampant with need.

"All for me?" she replied.

"Every single inch. I'll be up when you get off and I'll be listening to "Behind Closed Doors" by Johnny Gill.

"Thirty seconds, Brooklyn," Terry said. She gave him the thumbs up.

"My house or yours?" she typed.

"Yours. I need to hear you scream," he typed and Brooklyn was speechless.

How was she going to make it through her next three hours knowing what was waiting for her? She typed in the passcode to her door and the alarm and put her phone in her bag. The next three hours were about to be the longest three hours of her life.

Diezel smiled when he saw the codes. He had been up and sitting on his deck listening to her show for the past hour. Delia and Dani were both sound asleep. He was wide awake and thinking about Brooklyn and then to hear what her show was going to be about, he wouldn't dare miss it. He now longed to be in Brooklyn's arms. In them, he found peace and love. He could block out the world and focus on how lucky he was that they met and had such a close connection in and out of the bedroom. Tonight, after hearing her show, he needed that connection in the worse way. He looked down into his lap at his straining erection and knew that the only way to calm his body was to be inside of Brooklyn's.

With the code to her door and to her alarm in his phone, he got up and went into Dani's room first where he found her with one leg hanging out of the bed. Picking her up, he gently put her over his shoulder and carried her upstairs. He knocked on Delia's door and when he didn't hear her answer and assuming she was sleep also, he opened the door slowly and once his eyes focused on the darkness, he tiptoed over to her bed and shook her lightly. When she opened her eyes and focused, she moved over and he placed Dani in bed with her. He kissed Dani on the forehead and smiled when Delia pulled Dani close and they were both asleep again before he exited the room.

Heading to his own room, Diezel hopped in the shower and knew he should be asleep, but sleep wasn't on his mind. His woman was. The woman he now knew he was in love with. He couldn't wait to not only show her, but tell her.

15

Brooklyn prayed she didn't get a speeding ticket as she sped up Pacific Coast Highway in her white Maserati Gran Turismo MC with red interior, to get home in record time at four in the morning. She had the top down and her long hair she'd pinned up earlier was flying free in the cool night air. She had hoped the air would cool her overheated body, which seemed to get hotter the closer she got to her house.

After the hot text exchange with Diezel, she tried to focus on the rest of her show and after being urged several times by Robin to focus, she got through three hours that felt more like three days. In her last text, she'd given him the code to the keypad on her door and the code to deactivate the alarm on the house. Though she knew her imagination could operate on overdrive, she knew Diezel was a man of his word and was most definitely in her house waiting for her and she couldn't wait to see what was on the other side of the door.

Brooklyn exhaled in frustration when it seemed as if she was hitting every red light in the state of California. She was a few miles away, but the way her body pulsed with need, it seemed like she was states away.

"Come on!" she shouted at the light and then laughed at herself. Where had this kind of feeling for a man been all of her adult life. Just thinking about Diezel made her tingle and had her heart pump with love and not just the love of the incredible sex they had. It was more than that. Being with Diezel proved that what she had with Max wasn't love, but infatuation. She'd cared for him, but with Diezel, she'd fallen in love. Her heart yearned for him, her body longed to be loved by him and for the feeling of being wrapped tightly in his arms. She felt safe and secure, like she didn't care what was happening in the world because in her world with him, he made her feel like she was the most precious thing in the world to him.

A few nights ago, they had stayed up late watching movies and talking about what was next for them now that they were in their thirties. She loved that Diezel was ready for love with the right woman and enjoying a life with her having more children, traveling and he hoped to one day start his own law firm, though he was willing to wait at least ten years for that. He still had a lot to learn and when he shared his plan with her, she respected the fact that he wasn't going to leap into his dream without first learning all he needed to learn to make sure it was successful. She loved even more the fact that though with the kind of money he had, he could do anything, including not work, but that was the furthest thing from his mind. He wanted to show his daughter how hard work paid off whether money was an option or not.

She had shared that she loved her radio show and had no plans for the moment to make a change, though she was seriously considering taking her popular radio show to the premium channel television screen. When she shared one dream that she had never shared with anyone about wanting to write a book, he encouraged her to do it. He believed in nurturing all dreams and if what she was doing now worked for her, he was happy that she had a career that made her happy.

At one point during their talk, she'd shared with him the fact that she couldn't have children naturally, but that she wanted children one day. Diezel hadn't blinked an eye when he told her that naturally wasn't the only way to fulfill her desire to have a child. They talked in depth about all the options available and she loved how knowledgeable he was about that. He told her he learned a lot about adoption and surrogacy from a legal perspective while going through law school.

Without expecting to or thinking to hard about it, she'd fallen in love with Diezel and as she pulled into her garage, her heart felt like it wanted to burst open with love for him. She couldn't wait to get in his arms.

Getting out of the car, she opened the door that led

to the inside of her house and looked around. She didn't know if Diezel was in the bedroom or waiting for her on the first level. She didn't care as long as he was somewhere in her house. What she did notice was the light scent of gardenias. Somewhere, her favorite candle was burning, but she didn't have any left after burning the last one out a few days ago. As she walked further into the house, she could also hear music playing and her pulse quickened the minute she realized she was hearing the smooth, sexy sound of Johnny Gill.

Dropping her purse on the floor, not caring that she did, Brooklyn slowly made her way up the steps toward her bedroom on shaky legs that sat atop her usual five-inch stiletto heels. Tonight, for work, she'd worn a short, white jumpsuit, with a pair of black and white Jimmy Choo Bailey Logo-Web Sandals. The sound of her heels on the hardwood of the steps click, clicked as she walked, making the sound magnify in the quietness that surrounded her.

She reached the top of the stairs and saw a glow coming from her bedroom. On the other side of the door, her love awaited.

As she walked into her bedroom, Brooklyn could feel her rapid heartbeat in the veins that throbbed in her neck as her heart skipped a beat when she saw Diezel with a wide grin showing his pearly whites as he sat at the top of her bed, on top of the pale blue duvet. No way could she miss the fact that he was naked with his legs crossed at the ankles. Her eyes zeroed in on his bigger than life erection which stood at attention and waiting for her. Nor could she miss the fact that his hand glided slowly up and down his glistening penis, no doubt from one of the many oils she now kept in her bedside table.

During one of their recent lovemaking sessions, Diezel had introduced her to edible oils, coating her body with it as he licked his way around. When in turn, she did the same for his body and especially his hardened member, her breath hitched at the memory of the taste of the sweet strawberry flavor that burst in her mouth as she licked him from the tip to the base. The burst of flavor caused her to enjoy performing oral sex on him even more. He was, no doubt remembering that night as well. She went out the next day and bought additional flavors to his delight.

As she tried to control her breathing, she took a quick scan of the room and noticed the four candles burning on the mantle of the fireplace, giving light to the darkened room, only accented by the moon that was bright and high in the sky right outside of the opened sliding glass door. She could feel and smell the fresh, clean smell of the ocean permeating from the waters that sloshed around the water's edge.

She closed her eyes and tried to still her heart, not interested in a heart attack before she had her fill of the gorgeous man in front of her.

Finding strength in her wobbly legs, she walked

and stopped at the foot of the large maple sleigh bed.

"Hello," said softly. She didn't know if she was trying to sound sexy, but that's how it came out. How could it not with the sight of Diezel in front of her.

"Hello to you. I've been waiting on you," he said.

That voice of his, Brooklyn thought, where every word oozed sex.

"I see that and I love how you wait."

"And I'm not even tired though it's after four in the morning," he said, in a deep, intensely erotic voice.

"You're going to be tired for court."

Brooklyn felt bad knowing he had a big day in the morning, but she wanted him like she wanted and needed her next breath. Seeing him and hearing that voice that she loved so much, especially when he was really turned on got her juices flowing. She couldn't wait to get her now soaked thong off of her body.

"Trust me, I'm already happy about being tired in the morning, considering I already know why I'll be tired. You look beautiful as always."

Diezel eyed as much of her body as he could before his eyes again locked on hers.

"As do you and you're naked. That's the most beautiful sight for a woman to come home to and I'm happy I got to come home tonight to you," she said.

"Yeah, I figured I would save us the time of disrobing, though I look forward to you taking off your clothes very, very slowly for me," he commanded softly. He knew his words had the intended impact when he heard Brooklyn's breathing deepen with arousal. He tried to hold his own composure, but his heart quickened at a feverish pace while his hand stroked his member relentlessly, driving them both crazy with desire.

Brooklyn tried to concentrate on his words, but her eyes couldn't seem to look away from how his hand moved and with it, his hips seemed to be moving in a grinding motion. She wanted to leap on the bed.

"Well, I don't have a lot to remove other than this jumpsuit, my bra, panties and these heels I have on," she whispered like a purring kitten.

"Whatever you have, remove it slowly, except for the heels. Keep those on and only those. The image of you with those heels on with your legs in the air is making me even harder," Diezel said looking down at himself knowing it's where her eyes were, too.

Brooklyn's whole body shook with anticipation as her body vibrated from the deep, baritone, husky sound of his voice. There was so much sexual energy in the room and she was happy to be a party to it.

"You know what you're doing right now is driving me mad crazy and hornier than I ever remember being before," she said, now panting.

"That's the plan, baby," he said deeply. "Your hair is down," he added.

Brooklyn ran her fingers through it.

"I know you love my hair down," she said.

"Baby, I love everything about you and yes, it

excites me when your hair is down and flowing around your shoulders. I need to see it closer. Come around his way," Diezel said, pointing to the side of the bed where he would be able to see all of her.

Brooklyn moved with steady steps, not from the height of the heels of her shoes, but from the sheer magnitude of how turned on she was.

"I'm so nervous as if this was the first time. I feel so incredibly beautiful when I'm around you. You make me appreciate being a woman just in how you look at me," she confessed.

"You are incredibly beautiful and I thought so the second I saw you at my door that first day. Now that we're together, I want to be sure I never stop looking at you this way. I want to see you shudder and have that spark in your eyes that says you're anticipating the delectable things I want to do to you next. If you stop seeing this look, you let me know and I'll fix it. I may get distracted, but seeing your beauty will always bring my mind back to you. Now, clothes baby," he directed and when he licked his lips, his hunger for Brooklyn shot off like a rocket as he watched her pant like an animal in heat.

"Not the tongue," she whispered.

"Oh, I have a lot of tongue for you tonight and not just for you to see. I want you to feel it and taste it and trust me, my tongue is anxious to get a taste of every part of that gorgeous body."

Diezel smiled as Brooklyn reached for the zipper to

her jumpsuit and began to nervously pull it down. He could see he wasn't the only one in the room barely containing their need.

"Slowly baby," he said. "I want to get my fill."

Brooklyn felt an orgasm creeping up on her and all Diezel was doing was looking at her with that hooded, aroused gaze that made her entire body tremble. She gripped the zipper and as he requested, she slid it down over the swell of her breasts, over her stomach and to the end where it stopped right at the top of her sex. She was so hot, she was barely holding on. As she held his gaze, she reached for the sides and slid first one shoulder and then the other down her arms. As she peeled it off, she leaned forward and was about to slide it down her legs when she heard him speak.

"Don't. Let it sit right on those gorgeous hips of yours. I still can't believe I got lucky enough to not only meet you, but to fall in love with you."

Diezel locked eyes with Brooklyn to be sure she felt and not just heard his expression of love for her. "I love you, Brooklyn. I want to say that before we go any further. I've fallen madly in love with you and it's realer than real, baby. You hear me? It's more real than anything else right now. It's not just your beauty, but it's all of you, everything about you. I love you," he said again.

"I love you, too. I thought about how much I love you and how much I love everything about you. Neither one of us was expecting this level of intensity between us and I wouldn't change it for anything. I love you so much," she said and was on the verge of tears after hearing that Diezel loved her. She hoped they would be where they are, professing their love for each other and now that it's happened, what they were about to do was going to mean much more to her.

"Loving each other is a good thing because you are perfect for me. Right now, I'm looking at how perfect you look standing there with that look in your eyes that says you're already close and we're not even touching."

"I'm not sure I can hold out much longer before I need you inside of me," she begged.

"I know how you feel baby, but I don't want to rush this. I want every moment of tonight to be special because this, between us, is love. Real love. You know what I want?" Diezel said sliding to the edge of the bed and throwing his legs over the side while widening them.

"Me?" Brooklyn asked excitedly.

"Yes, you and I also want to see you slip your bra off and show me how hard those nipples are because I'm sure they could pierce a hole through metal they're so pointed."

Brooklyn unclasped the front closure and the cups fell away and to the floor.

"You know what I like. Caress them for me," he pleaded softly.

To say she was ready to shoot off like a rocket

would be an understatement. The look in Diezel's hazel eyes as he anticipated her next move was all she needed to see. As her eyes stayed on his, she reached up and cupped the large mounds in her own hands, making sure to clasped her hard nipples between her fingers and squeeze causing a moan to rise from her throat and escape through her mouth. She had to toss her hair back and forth to reign in her desire to let go.

Diezel stood and moved in front of Brooklyn and kissed her deeply.

"Rub the tips baby and tell me how they feel," he uttered against her lips as he used his tongue to tease the seam between her perfectly shaped lips. When Brooklyn moaned he kissed her deeper, this time teasing her tongue with his as he swirled around in her mouth. "Tell me," he said on a sigh.

"They feel hot and hard and I feel a delicious ache as all feeling seems to be centered on them," she said barely getting the words out.

"Really? That's where the feeling is centered and not here?" he asked suggestively while reaching down and slipping his hand down behind the zipper of her jumpsuit and inside of her panties. The minute his fingers slipped further down, he encountered her hard nub that had come out to greet his touch. As he rubbed it, he couldn't help but take note of how wet she was for him as her essence soaked through the thin material of the silky thong she wore. Knowing how excited she was for him drove him to slip a finger down even further until he slipped it inside of her body. With the other hand, he reached out to hold her up as she collapsed against him, panting. "You like that?" he groaned in her ear, while licking and sucking on the length of the lobe.

"Yes," Brooklyn struggled to get out. She had to reach up and hold onto his shoulders to keep from sliding to the floor in a heap. She moaned through the pleasure points Diezel kept teasing with his finger in her. The moment he slid a second in, she couldn't hold out any longer. His mouth was now on her neck, nipping her lightly and the dual assault had her letting go of the last vestiges of whatever strength to hold back that she had. Her head fell back and without knowing what to do with the feelings that were overpowering her, she screamed his name as her hips wound around the hand that was still giving her one pleasure rub after another.

"That's what I want, baby. You feel so good. I'm wondering what you taste like. Can I see?" he asked.

Brooklyn couldn't speak, so she simply nodded her head. Before her eyes could focus and her head could decipher what was happening, Diezel reached down and slipped her panties and jumpsuit from her body to the floor and picked her up, still with her heels on. She squirmed with pleasure when he laid her flat on her back on the bed and before she could prepare herself, his head was between her legs where his tongue then replaced where his fingers had just been.

She had no time to prepare for the onslaught of desire that flowed through her as Diezel lifted her legs up higher gripping them behind her knees and holding her there while he moved his head and tongue around and around and in mere seconds after her first orgasm, he was serving up her second one. The waves of pleasure that soared through her tipped her restraint and sent her flying once again, higher and higher and again, she screamed a few curse words in between hollering his name as her head exploded with like white lightning.

Brooklyn was still flying high when she heard the sound of the condom wrapper and not giving her a moment to catch her breath, Diezel placed her legs over his shoulders where he kissed the heel of her foot, down the back of her legs and when she thought he was about to kiss her most intimate spot again, he leaned up to his full height and taking his penis in his hand, he slid into her. She begged and pleaded while thanking him over and over again for making her feel so good.

"Your pleasure is my pleasure baby," Diezel said as his body rocked into hers, sliding in further and further with every pass in.

Tonight, was not a night of going slow, but now he was ready to give her the fullness of him. Lifting her hips a little higher, he pushed deep and rode her again and again while going between calling her name and moaning her name. He slid back and thrust forward again with a powerful stroke that caused them both to slide further up on the bed. Joining her, he braced himself on his knees and sank deeper into her, increasing the pace, letting her know that this is where they both belonged, locked together like this forever. As the rhythm he'd set with his hips increased even more, Brooklyn screamed that she was there again and he let her know he was right along with her as he climaxed and all the air from his lungs escaped causing his head to spin and his body to convulse with an orgasm so tantamount, he had to hold on tight to her legs to keep from collapsing. His body was no longer his as wave after wave crashed again and again through his body and on one last powerful scream and surge into her body, his body quaked again and again before he finally let go of her legs and fell on top of her, bracing his body on his elbows to not place his full weight on her.

After some time, Brooklyn was finally able to gather some words.

"Are we still alive?" she asked pinching him.

"Ouch!" Diezel laughed, but didn't move.

"I'm checking to be sure you're still with me. That was beyond belief. I had three orgasm back to back, something that I've never done. What the hell was that? You're going to be the death of me if we always make love like this. That was so incredible. This is why I can't get enough of you," she admitted, rubbing his back trying to help soothe his erratic breathing.

"You do this to me," Diezel said. "Sometimes just the thought of you does this to me and the good thing is I know it will always be this way. I love you, Brooklyn. I love you, baby."

"I love you, too and let's move this party under the blankets so that you can get some sleep. You have to get up in a few hours, more like two hours, to get Dani to camp."

Diezel moved from on top of her, going into the bathroom to dispose of the condom before joining her back on the bed. Sliding close to her he pulled her close into the shape of his body.

"I don't have to take Dani in the morning. After that crazy mess with her mother, she's spending the day with Delia. They're going to the aquarium and then some store where Dani can build her own doll or something like that. I told her to have Dani back by five in the evening. I want her with family tomorrow."

"I'm sorry you had to have that talk with Jessica. I could hear it in your voice when you called me about it."

Brooklyn had been asleep, preparing for the time she had to get up and get to the station and when Diezel called, she didn't care anything about sleep. The somber tone of his voice told her he needed to talk and so she let him get it out.

"I'm sorry for keeping you up when I knew you needed rest before your show," he said.

"Never apologize for any time you need me. If it's to

talk, if you need a hug, kiss or to make love, I'm always here because I love you. We're here for each other."

Diezel kissed her shoulder.

"You're right – we are and that's why I love you."

"It's fine baby. Get some sleep. What time do you need to get up? I can set the alarm on my phone."

"I have an afternoon court session at one and I need to be on the road by eleven."

"Oh, good. We have a few extra hours to sleep. Thank you for waiting up for me," she said.

"Always because you are everything to me. I wasn't sure if or when I'd find the perfect woman for me, and then there was you."

"Yes, baby. And there was you," Brooklyn said and that was all she remembered before falling off to sleep in the arms of the man she loved.

16

"Are we going down to the beach for the movie? I saw a note in the door that the neighbors had all pooled their resources and there was going to be a showing of a family friendly movie. I hear they're going to have popcorn, hotdogs, soda and other goodies. Are we going?" Delia asked with Denim and Dani in tow behind her.

"Where did you come from? I thought you were gone and that Dani was taking a nap," Diezel said.

"That's because you have Brooklyn on the brain. The two of you have been hot and heavy, not that I'm complaining. I'm happy to see that you're happy. I've never seen you like this before," she said.

"My daddy likes her. I like her, too, daddy," Dani said.

"I know and she likes you, too," he smiled and picked her up in his arms. "Do you want to go watch the movie on the beach?"

"Yeah, a movie!" Dani exclaimed.

"Then I guess we're watching the movie. It's going to be starting in an hour, so we need to get our chairs, blankets and any snacks in the house you want to take down there."

"Is Brooklyn coming? I can go next door to find out. I hope you remember she's allowing me to use her house tonight for a party and I want to make sure I have all of her rules," Delia said.

"I forgot about your party this evening. You're not planning anything wild, are you? You do remember I'm in love with her and I can't have my little sister with her wild party ruining that. I expect you to respect her space," Diezel said.

He wasn't sure why Brooklyn agreed to the party, but he knew that she and Delia had become pretty close and Brooklyn thought a nice little gathering would be good since Delia would be spending more time in Malibu and moving to the area in a year. A gathering would help her build a friend base in Los Angeles.

"Nothing wild at all. These are a few friends from my acting class. There will be no alcohol because first of all you know I don't drink even though I'm not old enough, I can't stand the smell and second, I like Brooklyn and would never disrespect her or her house. It's a small party with food, which you agreed to pay for and we're going to swim and listen to music," Delia explained.

"And those staying the night are only the girls, right? There are no guys spending the night," he noted.

"Correct. They have rides that are picking them up at two in the morning. You good with that?"

Diezel trusted Delia and if Brooklyn was fine with it, he wouldn't stand in the way.

"Yeah I'm good. You check with her and I'll get Dani dressed and take Denim for his walk. We'll put him in his new cage out on the deck so that he won't have to be closed up in the house by himself. I got him a new cage I'm sure he won't get out of," Diezel said and laughed when Denim barked at him. "Go ahead in your room and daddy will be in there in a second."

Dani raced off and took Denim with her.

"Are you in love with Brooklyn?" Delia asked before she reached the front door.

"Yes."

"Wow, you said that fast."

"That's because I mean it. I love her very much and I've told her. She's also in love with me, but I'm sure our love isn't a secret to you. Thanks for looking after Dani and helping me with her. I know that's not how you planned to spend your summer in California."

"Actually, it is. I'm also loving these classes I've been taking and I'll thank Brooklyn again for helping to make that happen. Even if I wasn't doing that, I would still spend a lot of time with Dani. I miss her when I'm away at school and since I don't live in New York, I didn't get to see her as much as you guys did. It's been fun spending a lot of time with her. I'll be going back to school soon and I'm going to miss her. You're going to miss her, too, when you have to take her back. When is that?" she asked.

"Too soon. I'm not as ready as I thought I would be. This is going to be hard."

"I know. What are you going to do?"

"Maybe go back to New York until Dani is older."

"No, Diez. I know you want to be with Dani, but there has to be another way. Jessica made your life a living hell and this is the first peace I've seen you have in years. I love Dani too and I also love you. Maybe there's a way for you to split custody during the year."

"I would have done that if Dani wasn't starting school this year. This isn't daycare anymore. She's starting kindergarten and shuffling her from coast to coast is not fair to her," he explained.

"It's not fair that you have to be away from her. If you go back, what about what you and Brooklyn have together? Doesn't that matter?" Delia asked.

Diezel knew it mattered. It mattered as much as his life with Dani.

"Yes, it matters and we'll make it work. I love her so much that nothing will keep me from loving her, not even the opposite coast. I'll figure it out. Why don't you go chat with Brooklyn while I get Dani ready and we'll meet you on the beach? Tell Brooklyn I'll have an extra chair for her."

"I was wondering how they were going to show this movie and it's still daylight. I see they're setting up large tents on the beach."

"The neighbors are like family here and I love that. Besides, this way the kids can get in the movie and still not be up too late, especially Dani. She's had some late nights lately. Soon, she'll need to get on a better schedule so that I don't give Jessica something else to complain about when Dani goes home. I can already hear her shouting at me for getting Dani off schedule," he laughed. For once, he could laugh when it came to Jessica and not scold. Being happy in love will do that for you.

"Okay. I'll check with Brooklyn and see you on the beach. Can I be in the wedding?" she asked.

Diezel turned sharply and looked at her.

"Wedding? What wedding?" he asked.

"The one between you and Brooklyn. You don't have to deny it because I already know. Of the five of us, you and I have always been the closest and I know the look that says Brooklyn is it for you, so there's no need to put off the wedding for years down the road. Get your happiness now," Delia said and didn't wait for him to answer. She walked out of the front door only looking back to smile and wink at him.

Diezel shook of the thought and then stopped and stood still. He could definitely see wedding bells in their future. This wasn't one of those things like running off to Vegas to marry Jessica. This love he had with Brooklyn was much more than that and when the time was right, he could see himself married to Brooklyn. First, he had to figure out what he could work out when it came to Dani.

"Daddy? I'm ready!" he heard Dani yell.

"I'm coming now," he said and rushed in her room. He already knew she was picking out something he would have to argue over not letting her wear.

**

Diezel put the last of the dishes away after cooking them a spaghetti dinner using one of his mother's many recipes for the meal made from scratch, including the sauce. Brooklyn had just come into the kitchen after checking on Dani who he knew was sound asleep. They had all enjoyed the movie out on the beach. When they came back in, he'd prepared a quick dinner and then got Dani ready for bed.

"That dinner was so good and I hope there's enough left over for me to take a doggie bag home in the morning," she said coming up behind Diezel and wrapping her arms around his body.

"You can have anything you want including another good meal anytime you want. How excited are you to be off for the next week?" he asked.

"It feels good to be off and not because I'm flying off somewhere. I get out of California when I take vacation time and by the time I come back, I'm exhausted and then have to go right back to work. I can't wait to relax for an entire week without having to catch up on sleep during the day. I thought of going to visit my parents, but my dad is at a conference and my mom is going to visit her sister in Maryland."

"How are they doing? It was great meeting them and I enjoyed shooting the breeze with your dad. He wants to talk more about my firm representing his company with all their legal contract matters. I think they like me," he joked.

"I was shocked that they didn't toss a million questions my way when I told them that I was in love with you. I thought they would reminisce about years ago when I ran off and married Max telling them that I was madly in love with him when I wasn't. My mother knew I wasn't and made sure I felt and heard their anger. They tried to accept Max, but he spent so much time wanting my parents to be impressed by him that they never were and at first, I was upset about it and then I understood. They can read people well which is why I'm glad they met you. My mom raves about you and asks about you every time we talk."

"She's a wonderful woman and reminds me a lot of my mother. I saw how Dee took to your mom and I hope that was okay with you. She misses our parents and she had less time with them than the rest of us."

"My mother adored her and Dani and can't wait to see them again. I really love your sister and she is exactly the kind of sister I always wished I had."

Diezel smiled.

"Obviously, if you trust her to have a party at your house tonight you trust her. How many friends are there?" he asked.

"Six, four girls and two guys, all from the studio where she's taking her classes."

"Did I say thank you for asking Max about getting her in those classes for the summer?" he asked.

To show his thanks, he pulled her into his arms and kissed her powerfully, none of that sweet pecking. He'd been waiting for Dani to fall asleep so that he could kiss her the way he'd been thinking about all day.

"You did and he was happy to do it. He owes me. We're not on horrible terms even though the marriage was tumultuous."

"I respect that about you. You didn't end up with chump change and he didn't squawk about the settlement and I'm glad that there is no hate between you after what he'd done, especially after you found out about the outside children he had with two women after you were married."

Brooklyn winced with the reminder of how insignificant she felt or how un-womanly she felt not being able to have children of her own.

"He was crushed when I found out and not because it happened, but because he knew how it would make me feel after we both knew I couldn't have children."

Diezel lifted her chin so that they were looking eye to eye.

"You know that doesn't diminish my love for you, right? I mean, wherever our relationship goes, that doesn't have an impact on how much I will always want you," he declared and wanted to be sure she could see the sincerity in his face and not just hear the words coming out of his mouth.

"I know and I love you for that."

"No matter how not being able to give birth to your own children makes you feel, you are a whole woman and never think otherwise," he reassured.

"Words my mother has been saying to me for years. I appreciate hearing that from you."

"Good. Now, do you think we need to check on Dee and her crew?" he asked.

He'd had a chance to check on her before the start of her party when he delivered food and non-alcoholic drinks. They were planning to hang out in Brooklyn's pool and grill, partying into the night. He'd already told her to keep the music down."

"I trust her and right now, with us having this time to ourselves, you have other priorities," Brooklyn said, moving so that she was facing him, straddling his lap.

Gripping her plump bottom, Diezel pulled her closer, snug to that part of him that was already rising to the occasion, a state he found himself in whenever Brooklyn was around. He accepted the hot kiss she gave him, allowing her to take the lead. He loved that she had no problem taking what she wanted and needed from him and right now, that was a taste of his lips. He hoped her next need would be exhausting his libido. He was growing accustomed to their constant need to connect intimately since a connection as deep as the one they had was rare.

"I love any priority that concerns you," he said in between sensual kisses.

"Up," she said and Diezel knew what that meant. As much as he'd like to make love to her where they sat, he didn't want to risk Dani waking up and finding him mid-hump. He would have to spend years explain that to his daughter He never, ever wanted that to happen. They have learned how to get their amorous activities on around her schedule.

Diezel stood with her in his arms and lips locked again with hers as he walked toward his bedroom and closed the door. He would only lock it while they were engaged and then unlock it in case Dani woke up in the middle of the night. She didn't do that often and only once since she'd been with him for the summer.

Climbing down from Diezel's body, Brooklyn slipped out of her shorts and panties, making access easier and quicker. She usually loved how he took his time pleasing every single part of her body, but tonight, she just needed him. She sat on the edge of the bed and as soon as he was within reach after removing his shirt, she pulled him close to her when he reached for the waistband of his denim shorts. When he tried to join him on the bed, she stiffened her arm, encouraging him to stand where he was. She leaned over and pulled a condom from the stash he kept in the table next to the bed. Setting it on the bed, she would need it, but not at the moment. First, she had another plan in mind as she carefully lowered his zipper where his erection stood proud and strong over the top of his boxer briefs. She helped him slide both articles of clothing down his legs and when he reached for her, she moved out of his embrace and instead gripped his aroused penis in both of her hands. Tonight, she wanted to turn the tables and pleasure him the way he'd shown her with a member his size. It wasn't easy taking him into her mouth, but she loved working on as much as she could. Not waiting another beat, she stroked him from base to the large mushroom head and when she heard his intake of breath, she covered the head with her lips, caressing and loving him with her mouth keeping her eyes on his to capture his reaction. When his head dropped back and he whispered her name, she knew the love she had for him was personified in how she loved him this way. They held nothing back when it came to the ultimate pleasure when they were together. He always made sure her needs were met before his own and tonight, she wanted to show him that she was an equal opportunity pleaser.

As she continued to caress him with her mouth and her hands, her body craved him even more every time he whispered her name. She could feel his body getting close as the movement in his hips increased in its pace causing her to give to him more and more. The moment she felt his rise up a little on his feet, there was no doubt he was on the brink.

In a swift move that surprised her, Diezel lifted her from the bed and after sitting on the edge himself, he planted her in his lap and grabbed the condom.

"You know how wild I get when you do that and unless we want to wake Dani when I howl like a wild animal, I needed to pull this back in a bit. I was close, so close, but I want to be inside of you. I love how your lips and hands feel on me and I'll never tire of that, but tonight, I want to feel you – I need to feel you, baby," he said putting the condom on.

As he was about to roll her over under him, Brooklyn braced her feet on the mattress preventing him from moving. Before he could object, she rose up on her knees and positioned his rock-hard penis at her entrance. Inhaling deeply, she slid her body down over his and focused on the feeling of how long and steely he felt entering her.

"And then there was you," she whispered against his lips as they loved each other. She held on, capturing his lips again and then releasing them slowly to lick across the seam between his lips from one end to the other, never losing the motion of moving up and down on him.

"You and me, baby. You and me," Diezel uttered and held on to her hips as they worked together on the slow, erotic pace of the moment. He let his lips slip down to find that perfect spot on her neck that he knew drove her crazy. He centered on it, focused on his while uttering how good she felt making love to him.

Brooklyn let loose a moan she couldn't contain holding back on turning it into a full-fledged yell. She remembered they were not alone in the house.

The smooth, slow rhythm they started with turned wild with exquisite sensations flowing between them. With eyes open and on each other, the moment was enhanced when he could see that Brooklyn was on the edge of her powerful release and he wanted his eyes locked on her the moment it hit. Holding onto her hips, he increased his upward thrusts, clinching his teeth when he felt her inner muscles gripping him tight.

Brooklyn felt the pressure building in her body and before long, she threw her head wildly from side to side and she rocked hard through a steamy, intoxicating release.

"I love you, baby! I love you so much," she whispered as she leaned her head into the space between his shoulder and his head, moaning through her climax and using his neck to muffle her erotic sounds.

"Yes, baby!" Diezel tried to moan quietly, but was losing his will-power as his own release slammed into him like an electric surge. He was glad his feet were planted firmly on the floor or they would have tumbled over from the impact of his turbulent release. Holding her closer as his body calmed, Diezel caressed her body, leaning down to kiss around her breast which were pressed firmly against his chest. He loved the feel of her.

"I'll never get enough of you," Brooklyn said softly.

"Neither will I and that's a good thing. I don't see a reason why we would need to," Diezel said repeating himself this time not with words, but with a kiss that relayed his thoughts as clearly as his words. He took his time savoring the delicious open-mouthed kiss while his hands caressed her exposed skin. Their lovemaking had been frantic and filled with intensity and now, he just wanted to hold her in his lap and enjoy the closeness. This is how he wanted to stay forever.

17

Brooklyn exited Dani's bedroom after helping her pick out the perfect pink outfit to wear for their fun day out. With one week left for her to spend in California, Diezel planned a fun day at Universal Studios. Brooklyn had spent the night with them after falling asleep in Diezel's arms first out on the deck where they ventured to after making love. Though it was Diezel's idea, she went along with it because she knew he was using it to do a check on Delia without actually going next door to check on her.

As they sat together on one of the lounge chairs with her sitting between his legs as they looked up at the stars, they talked about how their lives had changed since meeting. Brooklyn never imagined she would find the love of her life right next door. The past few months will go down in history as some of the best months of her life. They talked about their childhood and where they grew up. She couldn't see Diezel's face, but could imagine the look of shock on his face as she told him about growing up in rural Nebraska. That was when he finally understood her desire to break free when she met Max and he took her away from a life she found doldrum and introduced her to the limelight that was Hollywood. Diezel shared with her his life with his parents and she felt the pain of how much he missed them. She also told him that she could tell that he'd been distracted all day and she didn't want to get in his business and assumed his mood had something to do with business, he told her how far she was from the truth.

Diezel was dealing with the last few days of having Dani with him and though he knew the day would come, he wasn't ready for her to go.

Brooklyn felt for him because in the few months that Dani had been around, she'd fallen in love with her, too. They had done so many fun things together and she was excited to have been invited to the family fun day her camp held the week before. She watched as Dani excitedly introduced Diezel to everyone, some he'd met a few times before, but Dani felt the need to introduce him again anyway. She was one little girl who loved her daddy and Brooklyn understood why. It took her no time at all to fall in love with him and now she didn't know how to help his heart. She knew it was breaking with anxiety over taking Dani back and nothing she could do could soothe that ache. She wanted to be supportive and be an ear if he needed one.

In the light of day, he Diezel seemed even more somber. She wanted to see that smile she loved seeing.

"Are you going to be sad all day," Brooklyn asked, walking up behind as he looked out over the ocean through the sliding glass door. She knew he was deep in thought. Wrapping her arms around his waist, she leaned her head on his back and exhaled. Her life had changed so much since they'd met and she'd loved every single minute of it, including his somber mood.

"I'm sorry that it's noticeable. I didn't want it to be and now that you've mentioned it, I need to fix it before Dani notices. What am I going to do next week? I have to take her back and I don't want to. The love I have for her is unmatched and all I can think about is waking up and not seeing her smiling face in the morning or hearing her running around the house screaming daddy every few minutes. That sound is music to my ears," Diezel said, reaching down and holding on tight to Brooklyn's arms that circled his body.

"I can't imagine what that feeling is like. Being separated is hard and not just for you. I see how Dani is when she wakes up from a nap and doesn't see you. You told me what happened at the airport when she cried because she missed you so much and I know that was hard. You know, I've relegated myself to the fact that I will never have my own children and that's okay. I didn't always come to terms with it, but I have and then I see you with Dani and I wonder why I had to be the person who can't have children of my own. I see your bond, I see your love and that's something I'll miss out on when it comes to having my own child."

Diezel didn't respond right away. They had talked several times about how she was feeling when it came to not being able to conceive. He remembered when he first told her he loved her and she said the same. They talked about what a future for them would look like if their relationship continued to grow. Turning around, he pulled her into his arms and made sure she was looking in his face when he spoke.

"I love you, Brooklyn. You know that and I don't care if one day we decide to get married and we can't have our own children. When I told you I loved you, I meant it and that's knowing everything that I know about you, including the fact that you had a medical issue that prevents you from carrying full term. A bond between mother or father and child comes about from the amount of love you give them, not just because you give birth to them. I love Dani more than anything in this world and if we get married and decide to have children, I meant it when I said we can adopt, do surrogacy or even foster children. You are a part of my life and that means Dani is a part of your life. I have watched you love and care for her like a mother and I see the fulfillment that gives you. One day, you are going to be a perfect mother."

Brooklyn leaned back and eyed him.

"You've been thinking about us being married and having children?" she asked. "I'm not the only one who has had that on my mind?" she added.

"I love you and I see us married with many children and yes, I've thought about it. You are perfect for me. We enjoy each other, we hustle hard when it comes to work and play even harder when it comes to our time. I can see us building a life together and I don't want to be a downer, but I don't know how to have the life I want being away from her. I've been thinking about an option that I'm actually afraid to speak out loud because it means a major adjustment for our love when it's just starting out."

Brooklyn knew what it was. His sister mentioned what he was struggling with. Delia had called her to talk about some guy she was interested in and having only brothers, she didn't have an older sister to confide in. Once she told Delia to talk to her at any time, they had talked several times. During their last chat, Delia talked about how sad Diezel was about having to take Dani back and though others had been giving him advice about seeking custody from Jessica, she knew he didn't want to take Dani away from her mother unless there was a reason that meant Dani would be unsafe with Jessica. So far, that hasn't been the case. As much as he loved Dani, he knew that taking her from her mother was not the answer.

Delia mentioned that Diezel was going back and forth between staying in California and moving back to New York. When she heard the words, her pulse quickened and she remembered pacing around her bedroom while they talked on the phone. She had just gotten settled into her relationship with Diezel and she wasn't ready to give up her perfect guy. She wasn't a selfish woman and wouldn't turn into one especially when it came to her man and his daughter. She wanted what he wanted.

"I already know what you're going to say. You're thinking about moving back to New York," she said and leaned her head on his chest.

"I'm sorry, baby. I know what the idea of that means for you and me."

"Diezel, you have to do what you have to for you and Dani and right now, she needs her daddy. I see that and I understand. I've never had a long-distance relationship before, but you, my love, are worth every single mile I'd have to travel back and forth to see you and to see Dani. We'll make it work with whatever you choose. I am here to support you in any way I can. Lean on me when you need to and don't suffer with sad feelings alone. That precious little girl will only be this young for a short time and I know you don't want to miss anything. I wouldn't want to miss anything if I was in your shoes."

Diezel kissed her sweetly, pulling her into his body.

"That's why I love you and if I do move back, I'm going to keep my house I'm having remodeled here. I guess I would be a two-coast kind of guy. Where is that daughter of mine? Dani?" he called out.

"Daddy?" she hollered back and he and Brooklyn laughed quietly.

"Dani, my calling your name wasn't for you to call mine back at me. I'm calling you because you need to come into this room where I am," he said and waited. A few seconds later, she appeared smiling.

"Denim doesn't like the cage, daddy, so I was keeping him company," she said standing in the doorway, not quite leaving her bedroom, but enough where he could see her.

"I know he doesn't, but we can't take him with us and I don't want him running all over the house while we're gone. He'll be fine. Are you ready to go?" he asked walking closer to her as she finally exited the bedroom.

"Are we going to get on rides?" she asked.

"We are if you're ready to go. Brooklyn has to go next door to change and then we're off. Do you want to go with her while I make a quick call?" he asked. He turned to Brooklyn to mouth that he needed to call Jessica about taking Dani back.

"Can I?" Dani asked while clapping and bouncing up and down.

"Yes, you can," Brooklyn said. "We'll be ready in five minutes and we'll come back to get your daddy, okay?"

"Okay, bye daddy. I'm going with Ms. Brooklyn," Dani said, taking Brooklyn's hand and leading her to the door.

"Oh, just like that you're leaving daddy all alone."

"You have Denim," she said. He laughed at how serious his now five-year-old sounded. He still couldn't believe that two weeks ago, she'd turned five. To celebrate, they visited Disneyland where Dani was able to dress up as a princess and have a princess party. Besides, him, Brooklyn, Delia and Robin, Dalton had flown in from Florida for two days to celebrate. Dani had so much fun, he had to wait until she had fallen asleep to get her princess dress off of her. He was glad he'd bought her a princess dress in several different colors because she loved wearing one every day.

"Knock on the door when you're ready," Brooklyn said as they left.

After they were gone, Diezel was glad that Dani had gone next door with Brooklyn. He didn't want her to see the struggles he was going through with what to do to make everything right in his life. Even though it was a major decision, he knew his first day back to work after being off for Dani's last week, he was going to have to talk to the partners about going back to the New York office. No way could he stand being away from Dani for months at a time. The summer had been the best time of his life. He had Dani with him fulltime and there was no drama like what his life had been like back in New York. He'd met and fallen in love with a woman who showed him what real love was all about and now he had to choose between the two. Brooklyn was supportive as he knew she would be, but that didn't mean they wouldn't miss each other terribly being apart when love was in the air.

Exhaling, he took out his cell phone to call Jessica to first deal with the issue of taking Dani back. He would deal with his final decision of staying or not staying after they spent their fun day together. He didn't want anything to impact his jovial mood of having a day with his girls.

He dialed Jessica and said a silent prayer that the conversation didn't get heated. He was shocked that the day before, she had called him and calmly asked to talk. He wanted to talk to her, too. What he wasn't prepared for was having the conversation with his baby girl. He wasn't sure she would understand going back to life that didn't include him on a daily basis. He didn't have an answer, but perhaps he would have to sacrifice his wants and needs for what his daughter needed and that was him in her life consistently. He focused the moment Jessica answered the phone.

"Hi, Diezel," she said, calmly, surprising him.

"Hi, Jess. How are you?" he asked, going along with the flow of the tone.

"I'm doing okay. How's Dani?"

"She's fine. She went next door with Brooklyn."

"I listened to one of her shows recently. She's really good. I like how honest and personable she is. Are you happy with her?"

"I am. I'm very happy with her and Dani really likes her, too."

"That's good. You deserve to be happy and that wasn't with me was it? I know I'm full of drama and no matter what, I have a feeling that will always be me. When I hear Dani talk about Brooklyn and you, I know that you found the love you always deserved. I'm sorry I couldn't be that for you," she said somberly.

"Are you alright? You sound different?"

Diezel's radar was on full alert. Something was wrong. This Jessica he hadn't heard from in years, not since they'd first met. Their relationship had been purely physical, but he felt like he loved her and cared about her as Dani's mother.

"I'm fine. I wanted to talk to you about something."

"Okay," he said and sat down to listen.

"Okay, here it is. I've decided that I want to do something with my life and I know it's not too late. I want to go to college. I've found a really good job and I think I can go far if I had a degree under my belt. Working and going to school is going to be a lot and you know I love Dani. I haven't been the best mother leaving her with my mother all the time and hanging out night after night with my friends, but that's where I am in my life right now. I know how much you love

Dani and I love her too, but the love you and Dani have for each other deserves more than phone calls and facetimes several times a week. I want to take some time and find me and to do that I don't think I can be what Dani needs right now. I know that because every time I've talked with her since she's been with you, every other word is daddy. I know she's scheduled to start school next week and you were bringing her back on Sunday, but I was wondering if you could keep her with you."

Diezel stood up so fast he felt dizzy. What did he just hear?

"What...what are you saying? Keep her with me for how long? I can't do this back and forth with you. Dani deserves more than that. She deserves stability and school is about to start in New York."

"I know and you're not hearing me. I want you to raise Dani in California, though I want visitation, the right to fly there and visit her and for her to visit me here. I'm willing to give you legal, full custody as long as we can work out the visitation. I love her and I don't want you to think less of me as if I'm tossing her away. You're her father and I can't think of a better place for her to be."

"What brought this on? Talk to me," he said, almost pleading. The last thing he expected to hear was Jessica telling him to keep and raise Dani on the west coast, far from her. He had been thinking of changing everything about his life to be there for her and here Jessica was making a different decision for him.

"I know my mother hasn't told you everything, but I haven't been connecting with the best of friends and I've been drinking a lot and doing other things I won't say, but I will say Dani doesn't need to be here with me. She needs to be with you where I know she will have an incredible life. You are what's best for her," Jessica said.

Diezel could hear her voice changing and knew she was struggling with crying.

"I love Dani with everything in me and of course I want what's best for her. Are you sure about this? You're absolutely sure that this won't turn into some kind of custody battle and you'll change your mind?" he asked. He wanted nothing more than to keep Dani with him, but he had to be sure there would be no fighting.

"I'm sure Diez. Draw up whatever papers you need and we can go before a judge and turn custody over to you. I also know that means I won't get child support anymore and that's fine since you'll have her. I do want time in the summer and we can work out holidays. I don't want her to have to take that long flight all the time, so I would like to be able to spend time with her in Los Angeles if that's okay with you. I know you're saying who is this woman on the other end of the phone, but it's me. It's still Jessica. I've been going through something and my mother sat me down and talked to me like she never has before and believe me, she straightened me out. She also told me she had already talked to you about taking Dani from me and you wouldn't do it. Thank you for thinking enough of me when I never gave you that kind of consideration. She's right, you know. Dani should be with you."

Diezel was so excited, he didn't know what to say or do. He paced back and forth as the idea of having Dani with him all the time started to sink in. He would do it legally so that there were no problems and there was no doubt that he wanted her with him. No doubt at all.

"You're okay going to court to settle all of this? I can have that done immediately. I'm sorry because I hate to talk legalities, but I need to have temporary custody papers drawn up today and sent to New York to your attorney. Per the current agreement, I'm supposed to bring her back next week and I'm in contempt if I don't," he explained.

"I understand and I'll let my attorney know to expect them. Her contact information is still the same. Do whatever you need to do. You've always been a great guy and I'm sorry I didn't know it when we were married. I was still trying to be the life of the party and wasn't ready to be a wife or a mother and I know that now. Take care of our daughter and after we get all of this settled, I'd like to come out the week before Thanksgiving. I know you'll want to be with your family for dinner that next week, but I'd like to see Dani around that time."

"That's fine. Anytime you want to come here, you'll have an open invitation. I want you to have as much access to Dani as you want and I agree that she shouldn't rack up air miles as a five-year-old."

"Agreed. Our problems shouldn't be hers. I'd like to be there for Christmas if that's okay. I'll be on break from school and I want to see her face on Christmas morning."

"I'm good with that. Like I said, anytime at all."

"Okay, well, I'll wait to get the temporary custody papers and then I'll see you when the court date is set. Tell Dani I love her and I'll call her later today. Give her many, many kisses for me," Jessica said sniffling.

Diezel didn't know what to say. Hearing the sadness in her voice, he knew the decision to leave Dani with him wasn't an easy one.

"Thank you, Jess. Thank you."

"Dani is the priority, right?" she asked.

"Yes, she is and so are you as her mother. Never forget that."

"I won't. Thanks for being you, Diezel."

After hanging up, Diezel had to sit down in order to gather himself. His heart was racing and his mind was running wild with happiness knowing that he wasn't faced with having to take Dani back and being away from her. Gathering himself, he put in a call to his attorney back in New York to get him to draw up the necessary papers and get them signed by Jessica before the date that he legally had to return her to New York.

Diezel said a silent prayer before gathering himself and going in search of his girls. The day was looking up and he wouldn't have to walk away from his baby girl screaming for him in another airport. Neither of them would be able to handle that. He had to rethink what life would look like for them now that Dani was staying. That means getting her enrolled in school and making adjustments to his work schedule so that he doesn't become a parent whose child is in school all day and then with a nanny or babysitter at night. He took his job as a father seriously and it was his job to be there for her.

After getting life for Dani in order, he then needed to turn to what was next for him and Brooklyn. He'd had a conversation within the last week with Davis about where he thought he wanted to go with Brooklyn. He'd jumped the gun with Jessica and haphazardly married her and ruined their lives because there was no real love there. That wasn't the case with Brooklyn. He loved her deeply and he wanted a life with her, something he felt she wanted as well. The next move was his.

18

"Good evening, everyone. This is Brooklyn Hunter and I'm your host tonight for another segment of *'Bring the Real, Realness'*. I've got some good stuff for you all tonight and you know I usually start with a song, my favorite by Marvin Gaye, but tonight, my producer asked me to dive right into our discussion, so here it is. Tonight, we're going to talk about...."

Brooklyn's words trailed off into an unfinished sentence when she looked down at the paper. She had been given a new topic that she knew nothing about. She looked up at her producer, Terry and at Robin who sat across from her as they signaled for her to keep talking, reminding her that she was live on the air.

"Brooklyn?" Robin whispered and pointed to her microphone.

"Sorry folks. Our first topic for the night is finding love after hurt. The spin is we're looking to hear from our men tonight. Ladies, I know you have a lot to say about this, but we want our men to chime in and talk about whether they believe in trusting their heart to a woman again after losing out in love in the past.

Guys? Are you out there? You have a thought on this? Call me now or hit me up on my social media accounts and we'll read your responses for you live on the air. My producer is letting me know we already have calls on the line waiting, so let's get to it. Caller one, you're on the line with Brooklyn Hunter – what's your take on getting over a past hurt and falling in love again?"

"Hi, Brooklyn," the deep voice said and her eyes lit up. She knew that voice. She'd heard it so many times that she would recognize it in her sleep. It had whispered in her ear while making passionate love to her and that same voice had expressed words of love to her in the deepest, sexiest way. It was that love and that voice that brought an extra smile to her lips.

"Diezel?" she asked and looked across to Robin who was smirking. It was clear she knew he would be calling and she'd been left in the dark.

"Yes, baby it's me and I want to say hello to all of your listeners," Diezel said.

Brooklyn cleared her throat and shifted around in her seat. Only she knew that her movements were because of the sexy affect Diezel had on her at just the thought of him. Hearing him almost made her come apart and he wasn't even touching her. It was all about the imagination of what she knew he could do to her that had her needing him like crazy. Keeping her cool and remembering she had an audience on the air and in the room, she went back to focusing on the show.

"I'm surprised you're calling. You have an early morning flight to New York."

"I do, but tonight I wanted to share my thoughts on tonight's topic."

She didn't know what was going on, but from the looks on the faces of her producer and Robin, she was the only one in the dark. She had been thinking about Diezel, knowing he was headed to New York to stand before a judge in order to secure full custody of Dani. A week ago, his ex-wife offered to let him raise Dani. The somber mood Diezel had been walking around in was gone and a new breath of life was breathed not only into him, but into all of their lives. Now he was call into her show, shocking her."

"Okay, take it away," she said.

"Well, for anyone who doesn't know, my name is Diezel and that sexy, sultry voice you hear on the air five nights a week in the form of Brooklyn Hunter is the love of my life. I love her more than words could ever explain. Loving her wasn't on my agenda because I'd been coming off of a marriage that didn't work out and I was damaged from it. My heart was broken when I couldn't make the marriage work, but out of that came a little girl whom I love with everything in me. Your topic for tonight asks if we men think that after our hearts are broken, can we be open to giving our full love to another person and in my case another woman and I am an example that yes, we can. Like all of you, I knew of Brooklyn, I'd listened to her show and then I met her and found out she was much more than what comes across the air for four hours a night. She's kind, loving, gives her all to any and every one close to her and she's open to giving all that she is in the name of love and happiness. I was hurt for so long after my marriage broke down that I spiraled into one woman after the other, not making a commitment to any until I met Brooklyn. She changed all of that for me. She showed me that my heart was worth feeling the kind of deep, passionate love I have for her. From the moment I met her, I haven't held back anything including letting her all the way in. I think even if I had tried to close myself off from her, the incredible woman she is would find a way in anyway because she and I, ladies and gentlemen, were meant to be. So, in response to tonight's topic, yes, I think we could all find the perfect love after being hurt. I'm living that perfect life right now and I wanted everyone to know how much I love, adore and cherish you, baby. I'm heading to New York for a few days, but I take your love with me as I go knowing that when I return, you'll be here with as much love as I want and need."

Like him, he knew that Brooklyn struggled with finding the perfect love and now that they had it, he wanted to shout it to the ends of the earth. She brought a happiness back to his life that he never knew was missing.

When he had the idea to call in on her show, he reached to Robin who was able to convince their producer to lead off with this topic.

"Uh, thank you Diezel for calling in tonight. We're going to take a short break and we'll be right back," Robin interrupted. She looked over and saw Brooklyn crying and unable to gather herself and knew they didn't want dead air.

"No, don't," Brooklyn finally said. "I'm okay. Diezel, thank you for calling in, baby. You renewed my faith in love and I look forward to every day that I get to say I love you and to hear you say you love me. I agree, that the best love is a love you give your all to and open up to without any doubt that hurt will enter it again."

Feeling a little choked up, she paused and was about to talk again when she heard Diezel's voice. He was still on the air.

"I hope you'll feel that way fifty years from now because with the world listening in, you, Brooklyn Hunter, with millions of listeners on the air including your parents and other relatives, my brothers and my sister and other family, you are my greatest love and I would love it if you would say you love me enough to marry me. Will you marry me, Brooklyn, and make me the happiest man alive?" Diezel asked.

Brooklyn, shocked beyond belief looked around the studio and not only were Robin and her producer smiling like they'd won the lottery, Diezel appeared on the other side of the glass and behind him stood her mother and father, both with tears streaming down their faces, matching what she had no doubt her face looked like.

"To all of our listeners out there, let's welcome Diezel into our studio tonight along with Brooklyn's mother and father, Mr. and Mrs. Hunter."

"Mom, Dad? Diezel? You're here," she said.

Walking into the studio, Diezel walked right over to her.

"Yes I am. I couldn't propose over the air and not be here to put this ring on your finger once I got an answer," he said.

Brooklyn looked around mystified at all that was going on. The phone lines were going crazy.

"For those listening in, this hunk of a man is now on one knee proposing to our host. We want to know should she say yes? Let me hear from you on our social media accounts!" Robin shouted. "I see you all are blowing up our Twitter and Instagram pages, keep them coming," she added. "You're all witnesses to a perfect moment for our host. She gives us her all and tonight, she's deserving of every bit of happiness that comes her way."

"Brooklyn?" Diezel called.

"Yes! There is no other answer," Brooklyn said and leaped into his arms forgetting about the ring.

"She said yes, y'all! Our Brooklyn Hunter is an engaged woman. For anyone who ever wondered what qualified her to be on the air talking about love every night, this here is the reason why," Robin said.

"I love you," she said as Diezel placed the ring on her finger.

"I love you, too."

"Life for me was never this happy – and then there was you," she said going into his arms again.

"Yes, baby, and then there was you," he replied, pulling her into his arms and holding on tight.

**

Brooklyn crawled into bed just as Diezel exited the bathroom in his suit ready to head to the airport for his flight to New York.

"Are you sure you don't need me to pack anything extra for you?" she asked trying to talk through the yarns.

"I'm positive. Get some sleep because you've had a long night and you'll be back on the air tonight."

"That was some show last night. You got me good with that. I still can't figure out how you were able to get my parents to Los Angeles without me knowing about it. My mom usually can't hold water, yet she kept that from me. I see you're already topping me on her list of her favorite people," she said snuggling deeper into the bed.

"You can use that mastermind of yours and figure it out later. You need to get some sleep and I'll be back in three days. Last time, are you sure you don't need me to take Dani with me? I can still get a different flight to get her a seat. It's not too much."

"Diezel, we talked about this. She'll be fine and

school has already started for her. We don't want her missing any time in school. I just spoke to my mom and she said they're going to stay a few extra days to help out with Dani while you're gone. Did I tell you that each one of your siblings called me at the station to congratulate us after you left? They all listened to the broadcast."

"I knew they would because that's how we roll. We support each other in everything and me telling them I was in love and really in love was all they needed to hear. Besides, after my brothers got the rundown on you and then met you for themselves, if I didn't marry you, one of my other brothers would have tried," he joshed.

"Nobody holds a torch to my baby."

"You got that right. I'm going to leave quietly to not wake everyone up."

"Is your sister still here?" she asked.

"No. She left on a really early flight to get back to school. She only came to be here for my proposal. I had a different idea because Dani would be here and I wouldn't want to take her out that time of night breaking her sleep on a school night. When Delia said she would fly in, everything was set."

"And to think I fell for her telling me she flew in for an audition."

"Actually, she did have an audition and they offered her the role on the spot. Thankfully, it's a small role and she will only miss a week of school, which is fine with her professors since she's an acting and theater arts major. This is the kind of opportunity they're all hoping for. She got this on her own. What she didn't tell you was that she was also here for the proposal. I was able to get your parents here at the same time and so it all worked out. Proud of how I pulled that off? I'm good like that!" he celebrated.

"Oh, yeah, you're good like that alright. I'm going to miss you and I know the court situation is going to work out fine. You have all your papers in order?"

Brooklyn was a lot less concerned than Diezel was about the court proceedings giving him full custody of Dani. Due to the time sensitive nature of the situation and so that Dani would not miss any school, his and Jessica's lawyers were able to get a hearing where the judge would make sure Jessica understood what it meant to give him full custody and to also make sure she wasn't coerced by any means, like money, to turn over custody. When he returned, they could settle into a normal life and she was going to live out her dream of being a mother, even if it was as a mother figure in Dani's life.

"I have all of my papers," Diezel said walking back out of the closet and grabbing his overnight bag. "I'll be at the condo and hanging out with Dietrick for a few days while I'm in New York. Call me if you need anything and thank you parents for staying and helping with Dani. They're going to make wonderful grandparents to Dani and to all of the other children we'll bring into our family."

"I'm ready," Brooklyn declared.

"So am I," Diezel said.

He walked over and kissed her making sure it was the kind of kiss she would remember and hold on to until he returned.

"I love you," Brooklyn yawned.

Before he could respond, she had fallen asleep. Before catching his flight, he needed to run next door to Brooklyn's house where her parents were staying and in about an hour, will help get Dani to school so that Brooklyn can sleep. They were the kind of parents he knew his own parents would have been. He took one last look at Brooklyn as he used the remote to close the curtains, sending the room into darkness.

"And then there was you," he said to the woman of every man's dreams. He was glad she was his reality. His real, realness.

Epilogue

Thanksgiving Day
3-months later

Diezel whipped his head left and right watching Brooklyn as she flew by him going from the kitchen to the dining room.

"Baby, slow down. You're going to be exhausted before everyone gets here."

"I know. I want everything to be perfect."

"My family doesn't need perfection and I know your parents enough to know they don't either. They'll understand we just moved into the house and we still have a lot of unpacking to do."

Diezel looked around at their expansive five-bedroom house. The renovations had finally been completed and less than a week ago, he and Dani moved from Davis' house in Malibu into their own house and Brooklyn had decided that she would move in with them, though she was going to keep the house on the beach. That would be there getaway, especially since Dani loved the beach.

"Do you have to pick anyone up at the airport? I sent transportation for my parents. I did ask Delia, Dalton and Detrick and they all said they already had cars and would be here on time," Brooklyn said.

"Right and Davis is back and at his house. Except for Delia, the brothers are staying with him."

"You know any of them can use my house, which will soon be our house, anytime they want."

"I'm sure they'll appreciate that and the fact that they won't have to fight over Davis' house when they're here. I'm looking forward to our big New Year's Day wedding," Diezel declared. He couldn't wait to have Brooklyn as his wife.

"Me too. Your sister has been a big help even from school. I showed Dani's dress to Jessica and she loved it."

"Speaking of mother and daughter – where are they?" Diezel asked.

He couldn't be happier that Jessica decided to come and spend Thanksgiving week with Dani instead of the week before. He stayed out of the conversation between her and Brooklyn. Right after the court case, Jessica had called him to make sure he was okay with her having a talk with Brooklyn since she would soon be Dani's stepmother. He didn't have a concern knowing Brooklyn could handle herself. In the end, they each loved the idea of them being a blended family and raising Dani with two mothers. He was all for that. The growth he saw in a few short months from Jessica is the kind of happiness he always wanted for her.

"Jessica took Dani with her to get some last-minute turkey decorations. They should be back soon. I'm glad Jessica is here. She told me about some of the things she had gone through and that made me sympathize with her and how she came up with the decision to give custody to you. She told me she loved the role I play in Dani's life and that made me happy."

"I'm glad. It'll be great practice for our own kids," he said and looked to Brooklyn for any signs of discomfort at the thought of them not being able to conceive their own children.

"I'm excited and I'm ready. Thanks for being open and understanding. I never thought about surrogacy or adoption and I'm glad we're going to be doing both."

"The one thing I never want to deprive you of is more children. I know you love Dani and I also know you'll make an incredible mother to every child we bring into our home. Dani will love having a brother or a sister. Right after the wedding, we'll sit down and choose our surrogate," Diezel said happily. He was just as excited at the thought as he was when he found out Jessica was pregnant with Dani.

"You're sure you're good with two children right behind each other through surrogacy?" she asked.

"I'm open to as many children as you want to have. We certainly will have the room for them. "

Diezel turned when he heard the doorbell. Walking to it and opening the door, Davis stood on the other side. He looked beyond him hoping to see Lanie, but Davis was alone.

"Hey, Diez!" Davis said walking past him straight to Brooklyn where he hugged her tight.

"Uh, did you forget someone? Where's Lanie?" he asked.

"Not here."

Curt, was all Diezel could think when it came to the tone of Davis' response. Seldom was Davis short with him, but his response was pointed and he didn't like it.

"That's it, nothing else. You're gonna say not here and think that's the end of the conversation?" Diezel said coming into the dining room.

"I'm done with it, why aren't you. She's not coming, end of story."

"What did you do?" he asked.

Davis looked at him and then looked away.

"Diez, let it go."

Brooklyn excused herself and went into the kitchen.

"I'm not letting it go. You've been with Lanie a lot of years and I know for a fact she was looking forward to being here. What did you do? She loves holidays with us."

With his back to Diezel, Davis sat at the table and let his head drop down.

"She was trying to domesticate me and I'm not ready," Davis admitted and spoke so low, Diezel barely heard him.

"What? Are you serious? That's ridiculous. You've been together four or five years? What's the sign that lets you know you're ready?"

"Look, I'm not you. I didn't fall madly in love and now about get married. That life is for some people, but not for me. I had to take on a lot once mom and pop died and that was as domesticated as I wanted to be. You guys are now on your own paths in life and Dee is going to graduate college soon and move out here. I've been wrapped up in your lives and work and now I'm looking to do my own thing and Delaney couldn't understand that. She's ready for marriage and babies and not that there's anything wrong with that. You know I love Dani and I can't wait for you and Brooklyn to plan for more children, but as for me, I want to be a bachelor, hanging out with the fellas, dating, going to strip clubs and all the other things I haven't done being about work and family for so long."

"So, are you saying we were in the way of you living your best life and now you're taking it out on Lanie? That's sad and lame at the same time. That's more drama than those shows and movies you produce. You told me once that Lanie was the perfect girl for you. What changed?"

"We haven't been on the same page for a while. I haven't told you this, but we actually split up back in the summer. Remember when I came back to LA without her? We had actually split. I just hadn't told anyone," Davis professed.

"I'm sure she was devastated. You haven't heard from her?" Diezel asked. He could see that Davis was devastated even if he was trying to hide it, which he was.

"Not since we split up and I'm sure she is, but she'll get over it and move on in time."

"Have you moved on because you look like you've been through the ringer?"

"Naw, I'm good. I haven't gotten much sleep lately while working on a new movie. I'm good though. What times is dinner?" Davis asked, standing and looking around avoiding eye contact with Diezel. He knew if they locked eyes, his brother would be able to see that he was lying through his teeth. He'd been miserable since they split and was thinking of begging her to take him back.

He and Delaney hadn't had any communication since they split and he thought he would have heard from her by now. Surprisingly, she accepted their breakup better than he thought she would and much better than he had. Now that he was back in Los Angeles, his house seemed empty without her.

While he was still out of the country, she had come back and removed everything that was hers from his house and by the time he got home, he could barely see any trace of her still around. He didn't realize how empty it would make him feel to have her out of his life. He missed her.

"Go check with Brooklyn. She and her mother are cooking everything."

"Where is everyone else?" Davis asked.

"Dani and Jess went out to the store. Dee is on her way and so are Dalton and Dietrick. Everyone's flight has landed."

"Where is Davis?"

Diezel and Davis both turned when Delia came bursting into the house out of breath as if she had been running a race.

"I'm right here. Why are you out of breath and looking all ragged. What's wrong?" Davis asked.

"This!" Delia said reaching for the remote and changing the television to a news channel.

They all stood looking at the television in shock as a picture of Delaney and three other people graced the television screen. There was a terrible accident in Milan where Delaney had gone back to after their break-up and she and the other three people who were on the plane with her were all missing.

Diezel turned and looked at Davis whose face was stricken with grief so suddenly, he feared his brother would have a stroke. He and Lanie may have broken up, but the look on Davis' face said that he was still madly in love with her even if he refused to admit it. He turned back to listen to the newscaster tell the world that the plane had been reported missing a day earlier with the three models and a photographer on board. They were reported missing after they did show up for a photo shoot.

Waiting for any kind of reaction from Davis other than blindly staring at the screen, they were all stunned when he suddenly bolted for the door without saying a word.

Brooklyn entered, clueless to what was going on. All she captured was Davis storming out.

"What's wrong?" she asked looking between Delia and Diezel.

Without answering, Diezel grabbed his jacket and followed closely on Davis' heels.

Brooklyn turned to Delia for an explanation.

"Did you know that Lanie and Davis had split up?" she asked Brooklyn.

"I didn't, but I figured something was going on. I was home a few months ago when movers moved all of her things out. I didn't pry. What happened?" she asked.

"Delaney was apparently on her way to another photo shoot in Milan and the plane she was on has disappeared with her and three other people on board. It's been a full day and so far, they haven't found them or the plane. Davis didn't know. I heard about it on the radio while I was driving here. It's on every station and I knew it would be on the television, too. Diezel went after Davis who stormed out."

"Oh, my goodness. He must be terrified. I don't care if they broke up or not, I know he loves her."

"We all know that and I think Davis just realized it, too," Delia said.

Brooklyn sat the tray of food on the table and went to hug Delia.

"She has to be alright. She has to be and not just for her sake, but for Davis' too. I don't think he'd survive losing her," Brooklyn said with worry.

"This family won't survive another tragic loss. Let's pray that she's okay. I have no doubt Davis will use every resource at his disposal to find her. When he finds her, he'll have to put his love for her to the test and show her what she really means to him. She'll survive because they have unfinished business," Delia said as they turned back to the television to get the latest information on Delaney, Davis' heart even if he refused to admit it.

Get, "Putting Love to the Test," book 2 in the *Malibu Hearts* book series – January 2019.

Other Novels by Cheryl Barton

Bachelor Series
Bachelor Not for Sale
A Designed Affair
A Perfect Combination
Love at Last
Twelve Bachelors for Sale – Coming 2018

Amorous Occupations Series
The Artist
The Bookkeeper
The Chef
The Dancer
The Electrician

A Lovers' Heart Series
Heartthrob
Heartbeat
Heartbreaker – Coming 2018

Stand Alone Romance Novels
Holly for Christmas
Snowbound
Cupid's Arrow
One Wish
His Halloween Promise
Home for Thanksgiving
Holly for Christmas
A Better Man
Bossy
Un-Break My Heart
Love on Top
Take a Knee
Love at First Sight
My First Love
Black Love
A Younger Man

Coming Soon from Cheryl Barton

Advantage, Love
a novella

Professional tennis player, Leah Duncan's career is over after an old injury resurfaced, sidelining her dreams of being a number one tennis player. Changing her focus, she decided to redirect her attention to helping other young, aspiring tennis players hone their craft in order to compete with the best of the best.

Derek Bryant is a single father of two living in Compton, trying to make ends meet while nursing a broken heart after the wife he loved and trusted walked out on her family to chase stardom. Derek vowed he would never fall for another woman who cared more for her career than family.

Meeting Leah when his children are signed up for her sports camp, Derek falls hard for the beautiful sports star, but then his insecurities put their love in jeopardy and he's ready to walk away from being hurt yet again.

What Derek didn't know was Leah means business on and off the court and for once in her life, she wasn't going to give up on have something that means more to her than her career – Love.

Coming August 30, 2018

239

Love at First Sight

Can you imagine one moment you're living a perfect life with a perfect love and the next, an accident snatches perfection from you?

Brody Grey never thought he'd find life and love again, but years after a tragic loss and a trip to an exotic island, a woman he spotted on the beach reminded him that love was possible again.

Kimara Banks thought she and her husband had a forever kind of love, but a train accident changed her life forever. Never in her wildest dreams could she have imagined new life and new love after one chance meeting.

Brody nor Kimara were ready for the destiny that awaited them as they struggled with believing in love at first sight.

The Lake House

Summers together at their families' lake houses as teenagers are what Danielle Fenton and the boy next door, Gannon Wilcox, loved about being on the lake in North Carolina. They fell in love at a young age and then one day it was over after Danielle ended their relationship with no explanation. The only thing Gannon remembered was seeing the woman he loved in the arms of another man.

Years later, Danielle and Gannon find themselves back at the lake, in their families' lake houses, both divorced after unhappy marriages and trying to find their next moves. They now have a chance to get this thing called love right as long as they believe in the history and power of love found at the lake that was always meant to be everlasting.

Bossy

Cassidy 'Bossy' Bostic came from nothing, but knew she would be something. Pregnant and alone, she was forced to run from her past in order to have a future. Her rise to the top as the owner of a fashion dynasty is what dreams are made of, but her hard, icy persona could have her living a lonely existence.

Drake Montgomery, a rising attorney heading toward the political arena, has fallen in love with the 'Bossy' mogul only to discover it's 'Cassidy' he loves, but 'Bossy', not so much.

Can their hot, steamy romance melt even her cold, icy heart? Only time and love will tell.

Heartthrob – A Lovers' Heart, Book 1

Cade Weston, Hollywood's most eligible bachelor and named the world's sexiest man of the year, lives life at the top with a bevy of beauties at his beck and call, people providing his every desire and more money than any one person should have.

Callie Hurston struggles to make it as a stylist to the stars in a world where women are intimidated by her beauty and men are interested in her body and not her talent.

Cade thought he had it all until he has a chance meeting with Callie and decides to take a chance on her talent and ends up taking an even bigger chance with his heart.

Can the playboy turn in his player's card and give in to love?

Heartbeat – A Lovers' Heart, Book 2

In book two of, "A Lovers' Heart" series, Navy SEAL, Calvin Lymon, was about his country's business when he allowed himself to cross the line and his heart got involved resulting in a love lost. Injured in the line of duty, he fights to stay alive for the sake of his newborn son, Camico.

A new city and a new outlook on life were exactly what physical therapist, Ava Cortez, needed after years of living life alone and off the grid to avoid being detected by a madman. She never allowed herself to love anyone, especially a man, afraid she would be found out. When she's asked to oversee the therapy of a sexy navy SEAL, she tries to fight the immediate and intoxicating lure to a man who exudes more sexual potency than she's ever experienced. Can she forget about business and indulge in pleasure for once?

Calvin deals with the days of therapy that drain him, but nothing compares to the salacious, steamy nights of passion with Ava that are having the biggest impact on his ability to get back to reality until an old rival resurfaces and threatens his life and his loves.

Once and for all, Calvin knows he has to deal with his past and risk losing his woman and his son, who are his heartbeats.

Take a Knee

Professional football player, Kenrick Wilson, never thought twice about taking a knee in solidarity with his team to show support for a cause that was near and dear to his heart. He was applauded for wearing his heart on his sleeve. His greatest love was for Justine Banks, the woman who stole his heart years ago, the mother of his children and his biggest supporter. Even though he loves Justine with everything in him, he has secrets and deep-seated hurt that has kept him from taking a knee for the most important purpose in life, making Justine his wife. Can he let go of the hurt from his past to secure his family for the future?

His Halloween Promise

Dylan Kennedy and Savannah Eaton-Kennedy may be divorced, but that doesn't stop them from indulging in some pretty hot and sexy encounters.

A divorce decree may mean that their life together is over, but Dylan has a promise to keep that could bring his wife back where she belongs; in his life permanently.

Home for Thanksgiving

Firefighter Nicholas Sullivan is going home for the holiday after he was sidelined due to an injury on the job. Guilt over a life lost has kept him away from his family's ranch in Montana and now he's forced to face his past demons and deal with a self-imposed life of regret.

Veterinarian Parker Wingate's first encounter with the handsome firefighter was less than pleasurable. She sympathized with his hurt, understood his pain and before long, felt his love.

Knowing the holiday season is ending soon, can Nick go from living in love for the moment to allowing himself to finally live in love forever?

A Better Man

Phoenix Graham is living her best life with the best man, her fiancé, Carson Stone, heir to the Stone Tower Hotel Empire. Her perfect life is shaken up when a handsome, rugged and extremely sexy mysterious man moves in across the hall and she begins to see that the rose-colored glasses she had been seeing life through were blinders. She soon discovers that Carson was the best man for her until she takes notice of a better man and his name is Gavin Black.

What's a girl to do when the best doesn't get better and better is what she craves?

Find more books and connect with Cheryl on her website at www.cherylbarton.net.

About the Author

Cheryl Barton lives in Maryland and in her spare time she loves to read espionage novels, cook, watch Sci-fi movies, spend time with family and friends and enjoy Maryland steamed crabs.

Indulge in more romance and inspirational novels by visiting her website at www.cherylbarton.net.

Cheryl is a member of the Romance Writers of America – National Chapter and the Maryland Romance Writers.

Connect on Social Media:
Facebook
https://www.facebook.com/authorcherylbarton/

Twitter
https://twitter.com/AuthorCBarton

Instagram
https://www.instagram.com/authorcherylbarton/